PYTHAGORUS, NEWTON

AND

THE TALE OF THE RUBY

By Alison Rawling

Chapter 1

Pythagorus and Newton were twins. Pythagorus was born first, at 12 minutes and 12 seconds past two on the second day of the second month in the year of our Lord 2222. His parents decided that he must be blessed by the mathematical spirits which guided the universe and named him after the only mathematical person they knew - Pythagorus.

Newton arrived twenty-two minutes later, in such a rush that he caught the midwife and doctor by surprise. So much so, that they failed to catch him and he fell off the bed onto the floor with a bang. By the time they picked him up, wailing, he had a bump the size of an apple. Well, it could have been with a little imagination! It reminded them of the stories of Isaac Newton who first discovered the theory of gravity when an apple dropped on his head. So, they named him Newton.

Their parents had never been conventional!

They both weighed 6 lb. 1oz exactly. They had red hair and bright blue eyes and their parents were very proud.

Apart from their choice of names, there was nothing extraordinary about the twins' parents. Katie was about 28 with beautiful blonde straight hair (no hint of red there). Slim and pretty, she was a fashion designer for a well-known clothes shop specialising in jewellery and pretty summer dresses for teenagers. She was famous for her coral jewellery which she sold online from her website.

Their father, Tom was foremost an actor and a singer but when work was not available, he wrote plays and jokes which he tried to sell on the internet. Sadly, none of his plays had been published and although he fancied himself as a bit of a comedian, his jokes were always returned! It was lucky he was such a good actor!

Twelve years later, their hair was still red, but now tinged with silver. Their eyes were still blue, but speckled with green so that when you looked into them you were reminded of the turquoise depths of the oceans. Their eyes were just like their mother's.

Monday was to be their first day at school. Proper school! Not the little school down the end of the lane where all the children from the village went. This school was in a city called Atlantica, based in somewhere called Oceana. The boys had been asking everyone where Oceana was but no one seemed to know. Newton had asked all of the teachers and their classmates but they all shook their heads in bewilderment. They had looked through all of the maps at home and had searched on the internet but could find nothing. Pythagorus, working on the theory that according to mathematical probability, someone in the village must know, asked everyone else they knew but to no avail. When they asked their parents, they just smiled knowingly and said "wait and see" or "you'll find out soon enough" which just only added to their curiosity.

Even more curious was the way in which they had found out. Their best friends, Harry and Billy, who lived down the road in number 24 and 25, had received letters in the Christmas post from Westerly Council telling them that they would be going to Underhill comprehensive in Underhill lane in Overhill. This was a village just a couple of miles away and they had all cycled there in the holidays so they all knew it well. Their teacher was to be Mrs Rose who was round and red cheeked and always smiling. A smell of roses followed her everywhere. They were both very excited as she was supposed to be the nicest teacher in the school.

But Pythagorus and Newton had received no such letter.

2

A few days later they had been out swimming in the cove at the bottom of Cliff lane. They always swam there every day after school and every weekend no matter what the weather. They had been able to swim before they could crawl and to them it had been second nature.

It was their twelfth birthday and they had gone down to the cove as usual in their matching blue and green trunks and their blue towels with a picture of Ariel surrounded by fish. Their mother had designed them, so how could they not use them!

They had swum as normal for about an hour, chasing each other around the cove, diving from the cliff rocks and seeing who could stay under the water the longest. According to Pythagorus' calculations, he was winning 532 against Newton's 496. Newton wasn't counting as he just knew that he could always beat his brother in the diving competition. No one else ever came to the cove, so the boys would play happily for hours.

When they finally climbed out of the, sea, dripping with water and glowing from the exercise, they found them. Tucked into the folds of their towels, two turquoise envelopes with their names engraved on the front in gold. Inside were two silver cards with silver fishes ingrained in the cards which seemed to swim from left to right, and up and down as the cards moved in their hands, glistening in the sunshine.

> "Pythagorus Jones"   "Newton Jones", they read,
> School starts at 9am, 4th September 2234,
> Atlantica Prep School,
> Atlantica
> OCEANA
>
> Collection by eel at 8am sharp.
>
> Uniform and items required - See attached list.

DON'T BE LATE

ARTIMAS

When they turned over the card, a long list of clothes and other items suddenly appeared. The list got longer and longer as they read it, and if they hadn't known better, they could have sworn that the card stretched out in front of them as they read down the list.

If you thought the address was strange, you should have seen the list of items required. As well as the normal things such as pencils and calculators, the list included ½ dozen water snails, a water proof tracksuit, a pink (ugh!) leather harness for their sea horses Goldie and Koi (who!), two Octopus quills and a mobile shell with the suggestion that their parents paid for free weekend calls. And finally, a letter of introduction from Mr Neptune was absolutely essential or they would not be allowed to start school.

What had Uncle Neptune, their mother's brother got to do with it? He was a Professor of ocean life specialising in the speech of dolphins and lived most of the time in America. They were very confused.

Pythagorus and Newton ran all the way home to show the cards to their parents. Breathless and excited they fired questions at them.

"Mum, who are Goldie and Koi?"

"Dad, where is Atlantica?"

"Why aren't we going to Underhill school?"

"Why have we got to have a letter from Uncle Neptune?"

"Uncle Neptune will be home in six months' time and he will explain everything to you," said their father Tom. The boys could find out no more information despite their constant questioning.

When they had gone to bed that night, unusually they fell straight to sleep. They slept in bunk beds with Pythagorus on top. Newton had started off in the top bunk when they first got the bunk beds but for some inexplicable reason he kept falling out of bed and banging his head. After the 10th night, and an average of three falls a night they decided to swap over and Pythagorus had never fallen out. Newton still fell out of the bottom bunk on a regular basis, but as he didn't have so far to fall, the bumps on his head didn't get too big!

As the boys slept, their sleep was interrupted by strange dreams of seahorses and talking fish, of a city gleaming with gold rays under the sea where people seemed to be able to breathe but blew out bubbles as they spoke. Dolphins and water creatures so amazing and colourful played and danced in the sea. There were creatures with no names, and shapes and colours that they had never seen before.

The dreams came every night after that day at the cove and seemed to become more and more real as each night passed. Neither boy dared to speak of the dreams to the other in case their twin thought they had gone mad. This was the first and indeed the only time that they had kept a secret from each other.

The months passed and life continued as normal. Summer arrived at last and Pythagorus and Newton played football or cricket, and swam every day with their friends. Sometimes Harry and Billy joined them in Arthur's cove but they couldn't swim as fast, they were too scared to dive off the cliffs and, despite their best efforts, they couldn't hold their breath under water. It was much more fun in the cove when they were on their own. Every day when they came out of the water they checked their towels but no more cards or notes arrived.

They were very puzzled!

At last Tuesday, September 3rd arrived. This was the day that Uncle Neptune was coming for a visit. The boys awoke bright and early with the dawn and by 6am they were washed, dressed, had eaten breakfast and were waiting impatiently for Uncle Neptune to arrive. Normally, Katie couldn't get them out of bed before 9am!! But today was different.

"Calm down the pair of you" said their mother "you are going to wear out the carpet if you both pace up and down like that. Uncle Neptune won't be here until 2pm, perhaps later if his train is late."

"Can we meet him at the station?", asked Newton.
"He's not normally late." added Pythagorus.

"No, I don't think so," said Katie, "we'll wait here for him as normal. Why don't you go and have a quick swim before he arrives?"

The boys shook their heads. They couldn't bear to leave the house in case he arrived whilst they were out. After all, he could have decided to catch an earlier train and be early! So they played cricket in the sunshine in the garden instead.

At about two minutes to two, a sudden gust of wind seemed to come out of nowhere bringing a cluster of stormy black clouds. The sky went very dark as the sun was hidden by the clouds. A minute later, the clouds were gone as fast as they had arrived and the sky was once again blue and the sun shone. At the same moment, the grandfather clock in the hall struck two and the boys heard the sound of the doorbell ringing.

Uncle Neptune had arrived at last!

The boys ran into the house, tumbling over one another in their rush to be the first one to speak to him. At last, they thought, we are going to get the answers to all our questions that no one else could answer.

Finally, Uncle Neptune was here.

Chapter 2

By the time they had reached the living room, Uncle Neptune was sitting in one of the armchairs by the fireplace. Their mum was pouring him out a long glass of cold lemonade. Silky, their cat, who for some reason followed Uncle Neptune everywhere, was already in his favourite place - wrapped around the back of Uncle Neptune's neck, nuzzling his ears and purring.

Pythagorus and Newton rushed in, both shouting out questions as they both tried to jump onto Uncle Neptune's lap. Silky meowed, jumped off him in a huff and sauntered away flicking her tail as she went. Tom, their father, stood laughing in the doorway.

"Uncle, where is Atlantica?" demanded Pythagorus.

"Who are Goldie and Koi?" asked Newton, "and why aren't we going to Underhill School with Harry and Billy?"

"Yes and why do we have to have an introductory letter from you?" demanded Pythagorus.

"Boys, boys, boys, "exclaimed Uncle Newton throwing his hands up in the air and laughing, "give me a moment I've only just got here! Let me have a drink first and then I'll try to explain some things to you."

So the boys perched themselves on each side of the chair and waited impatiently whilst their uncle finished his cold lemonade. Their uncle was a rather strange looking man. Tall and plump, he had long reddish hair that seemed to stick out in all directions from the top off his head, even when he had just combed it! He had a matching moustache and beard that were tinged with silver streaks which shot out shafts of light whenever he moved. His eyes could only be described as turquoise, and as for his ears! They were more pointed than round and seemed to stick up in the air at right angles. He always smelt a bit fishy so he was not someone who could easily disappear in a crowd.

"Well Pythagorus and Newton," he said, "now that you are both 12 and about to start secondary school, the time has come to tell you where you really come from. But, before I tell you anymore, you must both promise me that this will remain our secret and that you will never, ever tell another living person what I am about to tell you. Well, ignoring your mum and dad that is!" he added smiling and he stroked his beard thoughtfully. "Can I trust you both?"

"I promise, I promise." said Pythagorus and Newton in unison.

"Go on, go on!" cried Newton bouncing up and down in his excitement.

Katie and Tom who by this time were also sitting in the living room exchanged glances and smiled at their sons.

"Well," he said, "well to start with you might have noticed that your mother and I are not quite like other people."

"What do you ....." interrupted Pythagorus.

"Shush" said Katie as she held up a finger against her lips "and listen to your uncle. You can ask questions when he has finished."

Uncle Neptune started again. "As I was saying, your mother and I were not born in England. In fact we were born in a city called Atlantica. You won't find it on any map although I'm sure you have already looked (the twins nodded their heads in agreement) because it is buried under the ocean in a land called Oceana, which is found under the Atlantic Ocean. It used to be on dry land a long,

long time ago" he said sadly, "but a comet hit the world and there was a sudden explosion followed by the greatest landslide ever seen. Atlantica, together with other cities such as Plympton and Carth and the surrounding countryside collapsed into a hole in the earth's crater which was immediately swallowed up by the ocean. Within a few minutes they had disappeared forever."

"But, the Atlantian people were descendants from a long line of magicians and mystics." he continued. "Just before the ocean swept over them and in record time, they used their magic and created a glass roof which covered the land out a material called Glycon. This stopped most but not all of the water from crushing down and destroying everything."

"Glycon is very special." he explained smiling at them thoughtfully. "You can see right through it from one side but not the other. So we can look up through the water and see the ocean and all the boats and fish etc. but they can't see us. It's blue and green on one side and clear on the other. It's stronger than any material you can find up here on the surface."

By this time the twins were looking at him astonished.

"They also used their magic to wrap all of the people in a special film which allowed them to breathe under water." he added. "The film reacts with the surrounding water and extracts the oxygen. You can't see it - it's just like another layer of skin."

At this point he stroked his arm as if to show them.

"Unfortunately our lands are still under water." he continued. "Our ancestors managed to filter out all of the salt and they built a special purification unit so that the water stays free of salt and is crystal clear. As well as the purification system, our ancestors also built a series of tunnels, shafts and lifts which enabled them to move from one land to another and between the different types of water. Over time they also taught themselves to breathe for long periods under water and as a result they developed special filters in their noses. It enables them to move around our cities through the water. In an emergency, they could dive under the sea water and hide from prying eyes. This meant that they didn't need to use the special film anymore."

"Is that why we have always been able to swim and breathe under water?" asked Pythagorus excitedly.

"Yes," replied Uncle Neptune smiling, "you and Newton are direct descendants of the Atlantians."

"Is that where the stories of mermaids have come from?" asked Newton.
"That's right." said Uncle Neptune smiling again.

"So why are we living here?" asked Pythagorus.

"This is because in order for our bodies to physically develop, we still need to breathe in the earth's atmosphere. Our bodies need the warmth and rays of the sunshine to grow properly and of course we all love the food that you eat! We can't get the same taste or texture back home." he added grinning as he spoke. "All of our children are born here and you stay here until you are 12, by which time your lungs and body are sufficiently developed, but not completely, so you are quickly able to learn how to breathe under water for long periods of time rather than the 5 to 10 minutes you can do now. You are also old enough to start to understand our powers and knowledge and use them properly."

"To conclude Pythagorus and Newton," he finished grinning at them both, "it is time for you to come home and start school where you will be able to meet other boys and girls who are just like yourselves. It's also time to learn some magic!"

"Will mum and dad be coming with us?" asked Newton.

"No." replied Katie. "We have made our lives here and I'm afraid your father can't swim in Atlantica because he was not born there. Also," she added laughing, "I am hopeless at magic!"

"I was born here in England so I don't have the same kind of lungs," added their father sadly, "but you will be coming back home in the holidays and when you are old enough you can decide which land you want to live in permanently. If you choose, you can live in both lands just like Uncle Neptune does. It will be like going to a boarding school." he added with a smile.

"How do we get there?" asked Newton who was now jumping up and down with excitement and waving his hands in the air.

"But I still don't understand." Pythagorus asked him thoughtfully. "Why do you have to give us a letter of introduction?" He was always the more serious and practical of the twins.

"As you know," explained Uncle Neptune, "I am a professor of ocean life however, I am not always based in America. I'm also based in Atlantica and I conduct most of my experiments from there. As well as being a housemaster at the school, and a grandmaster, I am also one of the elders on the Atlantian Privy Council and as such I am one of only a few people who can send out the invitation cards or write the introductory letters which bring our children down to school in Atlantica. Artimas, who signed your invitation cards, is the president of the Privy Council and also your headmaster. They won't let you into the Atlantica if you don't have this letter." he finished, shaking his head at them.

"As for how we get there," he said chuckling to himself "you'll have to wait and see until tomorrow morning. First, we have to check that your suitcases are properly packed. I've brought some of the items you can't buy up here with me in my bags so it shouldn't take long to finish packing. Provided, of course your mum has done her shopping properly!" He grinned at Katie as he said this.

With that, Neptune got up and went to collect his belongings, with Silky following close behind, wistfully hoping that he had brought some fish for her! For the next few hours Neptune helped Katie and the twins check and then pack their suitcases. The extra items that he had brought with him included the two pink leather harnesses for Goldie and Koi (they still didn't know who they were and he wouldn't tell them!). Each harness had the name of the twin emblazoned in gold on the front but luckily the colour of the leather wasn't too pink!

There was also a pencil case full of octopus quills which looked similar to feather quills but according to the instructions they had their own inbuilt ink supply. The mobile shells which smelt a bit fishy turned out to be the equivalent of a mobile phone with Internet and Skype except that they were only connected to the extra one that was to be left at home so they could speak to their parents whenever they wanted to.

With all of the extra things that Neptune had given them there was only just enough room in their suitcases to pack all of their things.

Katie then placed their uniforms, which were two turquoise waterproof jackets, a T-shirt and a matching pair of blue trousers with leather belts on top of their sealed suitcases. Their father then placed two daggers on top of the belts with Pythagorus and Newton inscribed in very unusual italic writing on the silver blades.

"These are a leaving present to you both from your mother and I," he said "but be very careful with them." he added suddenly sounding serious.

"Wow." they both said in unison as the picked up the daggers admiring them as they glistened in the fading sunlight. "Thanks mum. Thanks dad" and both boys gave their parents a big hug.

Finally, Uncle Neptune handed them both two turquoise envelopes with their names engraved in gold on the front. They were exactly the same as the two envelopes that had contained their original invitation cards.

"Here are your introductory letters," he said solemnly. "I suggest you put them in the inside pockets of your jackets. Whatever you do, don't lose them!" he added sternly. "Now I think it's time you both went to bed because we have a long day ahead of us tomorrow."

With that he waited until Pythagorus and Newton had got undressed and climbed into their beds before saying good night. As their parents gave them a hug and a kiss, the twins continued to ask them questions, but they could get no further answers. Within a few minutes however they were both sound asleep, dreaming again of a city under the ocean.

The next morning, Pythagorus and Newton were up again at the crack of dawn. By 6.30 they were already dressed in their new clothes and had eaten breakfast. They then spent the next hour saying goodbye both to their parents and Silky. That is, when they could drag him away from their Uncle Neptune's neck!

At 7.45 the whole family left the house to walk down towards Arthur's cove to catch their train. Pythagorus and Newton were both a bit confused by that but thought that maybe they had to catch a boat first. To their surprise, Harry and Billy were waiting at the front gate to wish them good luck.

"See you at Christmas." Harry said, "And don't forget to send us a postcard." added Billy. They stood at the gate and waved them goodbye as they walked off towards the cove, dragging their cases behind them.

"Crumbs." whispered Pythagorus to Newton "How on earth do you think we can manage that?" Newton shrugged his shoulders.

Chapter 3

As they walked down the lane towards the cove, a sudden gust of wind came from out of nowhere and just like the day before the wind brought a cluster of dark rain clouds over their heads. As they climbed down the steep cliff path, the twins thought that they could see a dark shape in the water below, which grew bigger and longer as they got nearer to the beach. When they finally reached the water's edge, to their surprise the dark shape suddenly lifted itself almost completely out of the water, so that part of it was resting on the sand.

"Welcome to our private carriage." said Uncle Neptune pointing to the long black creature before them with what looked like a box on its back.

"What is it?" asked Newton who by now was partly hiding behind his mother and looking very unsure.

"It" laughed Uncle Neptune "is in fact an electric eel called Ellie and she is an Eel Express. We will be travelling in some comfort today as she is carrying a conga carriage in our honor. That is the equivalent of first class in Oceana." he added.

Ellie, who must have been at least 50ft long, had three large humps on her back. When she heard Uncle Neptune speak she lifted up her head and looking in their direction made a strange tinkling sound that they instinctively knew was a greeting. She looked just like the pictures they had seen on the internet of the Loch Ness monster, only much bigger!! Her skin was the colour of black velvet and it was covered in tiny water droplets which were now gently sliding down her back, glistening in the morning sun. Her eyes were bright red and her mouth seemed to curve upwards at the sides. She looked like she was smiling and seemed quite friendly when you got close up to her.

The conga carriage sat on a frame in between two of her humps. One minute the frame looked like a piece of red velvet and the next, as if it was made of silver. The carriage itself had a small door and two large windows on either side. The roof looked like it was made of blue glass but in actual fact it was glycon. On one side were painted the words "Conga Carriage" in turquoise (turquoise was obviously the Atlantians favourite colour!). The frame was then attached to Ellie's back with two pink leather straps dotted with pearls which caught the sunlight every time she moved.

Now just follow me and hurry up or we'll be late." Uncle Neptune told them. With that he picked up his bags and walked up to Ellie. As he approached her, she bent her head down until it touched the ground and Uncle Neptune jumped up and clambered up to the top of her neck. He then walked along her back, opened the door to the carriage and climbed in. A moment later he popped his head around the doorway and shouted "Come on boys or we are going to be really late and Artimas will be cross. He hates it if his pupils are late on their first day!"

Pythagorus and Newton looked at each other and gave each other encouraging glances. They then picked up their suit cases and approached the eel. Just as before, she bent her head to touch the ground. "Don't be frightened," she whispered in a soft silvery voice, "you'll soon get used to this. Just jump on my neck and head towards my back and the carriage. You'll be quite safe."

With no further hesitation the boys clambered up onto her neck, and then gingerly walked down her back towards the carriage doorway. Newton was holding out both of his arms and looked like he was walking along a tightrope.

"Good luck!" shouted their father waving.

"Take care!" shouted their mother in a tearful voice. "Ring us when you get there."

The twins turned and waved, opened the carriage doorway and then they were gone.

Inside the carriage; which was much bigger than it looked from the outside; were a number of comfortable chairs, a bar and a television. The boys sat down next to one of the windows and looked back at the beach where their parents were standing waving goodbye. As soon as they had sat down, Ellie slipped back into the sea with a swish of her tail and their extraordinary journey to Atlantica had begun. Back in Arthur's cove the cluster of rain clouds disappeared as quickly as they had come and the sun started to shine again. The sea waters became calm, and it was as if nothing had happened. Their parents turned away from the sea and slowly walked back up the beach towards the cliff path, hand in hand.

"Put on your seat belts," instructed Uncle Neptune "it's going to get a bit bumpy soon as we are going to hit the Atlantic stream in about five minutes. But first, go and get yourselves a lemonade from the bar.

"Quickly now!" he added.

The twins did as they were told and then sat down beside him gazing out of both the windows and the roof in astonishment as Ellie dived deeper and deeper into the sea. Strangely, the roof was now transparent from inside the carriage and so they had a wonderful view! As Ellie swam quietly through the water she left trailing behind her a silvery electric imprint in the shape of radio waves, so they could see where they had been and lots of tiny bubbles.

As they continued on their journey they passed many shoals of fish and dolphins and other sea creatures they had never seen before. If they hadn't known better, they could have sworn that they all said hello or waved with their fins or tails as they swam past Ellie. Soon the sea got darker and darker until they could see nothing but water around them. They continued to dive like this for about an hour before they started to see a glimmer of light ahead in the distance.

"Look, that's the light from Atlantica!" exclaimed Uncle Neptune smiling, "It won't be long now."

The light grew brighter and brighter as they approached the city. Ellie slowed down and then suddenly without any warning dived steeply down towards the ocean floor. She dropped into a hole which earlier had been hidden from view and then entered through a doorway into a long tunnel which stretched out into the distance. At the end of the tunnel was a sentry box, but when the guards saw Neptune, they just waved Ellie straight through. They then passed through a couple of large rooms and then another long tunnel before they finally entered the waters of Oceana. By this time, the waters around them were light rather than dark and had become crystal clear.

"That must be one of the tunnels Uncle Neptune mentioned." whispered Pythagorus to Newton, as they left the tunnels behind them and entered into an empty stretch of water. They then headed towards the lights in the distance.

About thirty minutes later, they approached the outskirts of a city which Neptune told them was called Atlantica. Soon they could make out spires and rooftops and buildings which seemed to be covered in gold and precious stones and which shone in the watery light with a multitude of colours. As they got closer the outline of streets appeared below them and then they could see moving shapes which looked very much like people.

A few minutes later Ellie dropped down in a final steep dive and approached what appeared to be a courtyard in the centre of a large grand white building with a blue painted roof at the edge of the city. The building looked just like a French chateau with lots of turrets on the roof, little diamond shaped windows and an arched walkway all the way around the courtyard.

"Here we are at last." said Uncle Neptune "This is Atlantica Prep school," and he pointed to the name painted in gold high on top of one of the walls underneath a tall clock tower. The twins were too stunned to speak at this point, but believe me their silence didn't last long!

Ellie finally landed with a thump right in the centre of the courtyard in front of a large oak door labelled "School entrance".

"Time to get out." said Uncle Neptune picking up his bags. "And don't forget to thank Ellie as you leave."

"I'm sure I've dreamt of this place." whispered Newton to Pythagorus as they picked up their cases.

"Me too." whispered Pythagorus back.

"Wow." they both said in unison, as they looked at each other in astonishment.

"Now," said Uncle Neptune sternly, "before we go any further there is something very important I must tell you both. You must take three big mouthfuls of air before you leave the carriage. You must then walk across the courtyard to the door which I shall open for you. Once we are inside and I've closed the door you will see that we are in a vacuumed chamber. Once the water has been drained off, we can open the inner door and then we can enter the school!"

"Whatever you do," he said wagging a finger at them.

"DON'T TRY TO SWIM to the door or you will find yourself heading back up towards the ocean and then we'll have to come and catch you! Walking on this land is not as easy as sounds, and you'll be taught how to travel around Atlantica safely in one of your first lessons. Is that OK?" he added smiling.

They both nodded their heads in agreement.

"That sounds easy." whispered Newton to Pythagorus.

"Now don't forget to hold your breath under the water, just like when you swim in the cove until we've gone through the door." instructed Uncle Neptune. "Are you ready?"

"Yes," they again chimed in unison "we're ready."

"Right," he said "let's go and remember you must try to walk. Don't run or jump" he added as he picked up his bags and opened the carriage door. He then jumped out and slid down Ellie's back and neck before landing on his feet on the floor. He patted Ellie on the head goodbye, and then walked with springy steps towards the door. He looked just like Neil Armstrong when he first walked on the moon!

Pythagorus and Newton took three deep breaths as instructed, picked up their bags and followed him out of the carriage, Pythagorus first. They also tried to slide down Ellie's back but instead of landing on their feet, Pythagorus slid down and landed on his bottom whilst Newton fell completely off and landed flat on his back!

When they entered the clear water they seemed to immediately lose their sense of balance as they had lost the gravitational pull that keeps us on the ground rather than disappearing up into space. With each step they took, the urge to jump up into the water increased as their steps, without even trying, turned into gigantic leaps.

Pythagorus, who had left the carriage first, quickly made it to the open door where he joined his uncle.

After three steps however, Newton found that he couldn't resist the urge to just let go and he soon found himself floating upwards, getting faster and faster, and higher and higher as he took each step.

"Newton!" he heard his uncle shouting in the distance. "Come back down here right now. Try and push yourself back down to the floor."

But try as he might Newton just couldn't stop himself from getting higher and higher. Then, as he passed above the clock tower, and just as he was starting to get a bit worried, Ellie jumped up towards him and grabbed his trousers in her teeth. She then pulled him back down gently towards the floor and placed him in front of his uncle who was standing in the doorway with a gentle nudge.

"I told you to be careful!" scolded his uncle, "Now hurry up or you'll find yourself running out of air." With that, he quickly ushered Newton into the chamber.

Neptune hurriedly closed the door behind them with a large thud and then pressed a silver knob on the side of the wall marked "Vacuum". There was another knob underneath marked "Water".

As the seconds passed, the twins started to become quite desperate for air but immediately after Neptune pressed the knob, there was a strange grinding noise and the floor beneath them moved apart slightly to reveal lots of small holes. As they peered down the holes they caught a glimpse of two large drains, down which the water quickly disappeared. Soon they were left standing in the chamber, empty now except for air and of course themselves.

Somehow, they were also bone dry.

"Welcome to your new school." said Uncle Neptune smiling as he opened the inner door with a big wave of his arms.....

Chapter 4

As the boys looked through the door into the school, an amazing spectacle greeted their eyes. Amazing because it looked so ordinary and they had expected to see something quite extraordinary. They weren't however too disappointed.

The doorway opened into a large panelled hallway with a beautiful oak staircase leading up towards the floor above. The staircase started narrow at the bottom, but got wider as it went upwards. It was a grand staircase. Hanging high above them was the biggest chandelier they had ever seen, which sparkled in the watery light sending arrows of silver light chasing each other across the walls as it swayed to and fro. It was quite strange to see the shapes darting around the room.

To the left and right of the hallway, were two archways and the twins could see two long corridors filled with many doorways stretching as far as they could see into the distance, and leading away from the hallway. In front of them and on either side of the staircase were two smaller doorways, one marked "Headmaster" and the other one marked "Matron" in gold italic writing.

What was extraordinary however, was the fact that the staircase, the corridors and indeed the hallway were filled with children of about their age and just older. They were rushing along laughing, talking and calling to each other as they hurried off in various directions. They were all talking in a multitude of languages, but the twins felt they could still understand every word they said. They had never expected to see so many other children who were obviously just like themselves. Some of the children called out greetings to Neptune as they rushed past them. Others waved or nodded their heads but a lot of them just ignored them.

Uncle Neptune swept all of the children out of the way with a wave of his arms and led the twins towards the headmaster's room. He didn't knock on the door as they had expected, but just marched straight in.

"Good morning Artimas," he called out as he strode through the door, "and that's "Headmaster" to you boys in the future." he added in a quieter voice. "I've bought Pythagorus and Newton to meet you. Katie's children if you remember?"

Artimas was standing behind his desk, leaning on his leather chair and gazing out of one of his windows through the water towards the city. He was surrounded by bookshelves which stretched from the floor to the ceiling and were filled with books and some strange looking objects. Strangely his desk was quite empty! He was a tall and lanky man, but he didn't look at all like a wizard or magician which was what they had been expecting. Instead he looked quite ordinary from behind as he was wearing a black suit, no hat and his hair was a normal brown colour. The suit did however have coat tails.

For a moment they were quite disappointed...

But when Artimas heard their uncle speak he turned around and then they were no longer disappointed! Where from behind his hair was brown, from the front it was now bright silver and yes he did have a beard but it was a goatee beard and not a long one. His suit was no longer black, but turquoise and underneath it they could just about see a silver shirt and a gold waistcoat. From close up they realised that they were all made from a silk like material, not dissimilar to the fabric of their own clothes but obviously more expensive. His eyes were the same colour as their own and his ears were pointed just like Neptune's.

"WELCOME to Atlantica Prep School." he said in a loud and deep voice opening his arms out towards them in greeting. "I've been so looking forward to meeting you both and now you are here at last. Oh, and you both have your mother's eyes." He shook their hands in greeting. "Have you got your invitations?"

"Greetings Neptune." he said turning towards their uncle and giving him a kiss on each of his cheeks.

How weird the twins thought!

"You are late Neptune and the school bell will be ringing shortly for the opening assembly, but I think we still have just enough time for me to show the boys around the school, but we must hurry. Come along now." he added and with that he picked up his staff which he used as a walking stick and marched out of the room at a brisk pace. He then headed down the left hand corridor without a backward glance. He was quite a sight!

"These are the classrooms for the senior school," he told them pointing to all the doors along the first corridor. On closer inspection, all these doors appeared to be painted red. They then climbed up a staircase which was situated at the end of the corridor and then walked back the way they had come. "And these are your classrooms." he said pointing to the doors which were painted blue.

At the end of this corridor, they walked over the grand staircase and headed along the right hand corridor. They passed more blue doors which were also junior school classrooms, came back down another staircase (identical to the first one) and headed back past more senior school classrooms.

"All these corridors and doors are going to be very confusing," whispered Newton to Pythagorus. "I'm sure we are going to get lost!"

"Nonsense," replied Pythagorus "I'm sure it's just a matter of logic."

Back in the main hall again, they headed up the grand staircase and this time headed away from the courtyard and straight ahead along another long corridor (with more unidentified classrooms) until they came to another identical staircase leading back down to the lower level. There were two more corridors on the first floor with green doors which they didn't enter as these were the teacher's quarters.

This time they stopped for a few seconds at the bottom of the staircase in order for Artimas to catch his breath. "The corridor on the left is where the seniors sleep, and this one on the right is where the juniors, including yourselves sleep."

With that Artimas marched off again until he came to room 101. "And this is your study room" he said as he pushed open the door and led them in.

Inside, the room, which oddly was much larger than the door and corridor had indicated; was designed as a bedroom and study combined for two pupils. The walls were painted lilac and blue depending on the angle you looked at them. Each pupil had their own bed, wardrobe, chest of drawers and a desk all made out of pine, with plenty of room to store all their books. Not that they had any books at the moment! In front and slightly to the left was their own en-suite bathroom including a shower and a bath.

To the right, and opening into an adjacent larger room was a shared sitting room with sofas, a table, a fridge and even a television screen attached to one of the walls. There were three other doors leading off from this room into three other studies. Quite how three other study rooms all built along a straight corridor could all meet in this sitting room was something that would puzzle them later and for many years to come, but at this point in time just seemed so logical! There were however, no windows in any of the rooms.

Pythagorus and Newton were very, very impressed!

"Come along," said Artimas, "just leave your suitcases here for now. You just haven't got time to start unpacking them now. You'll have to sort them out later as the opening Assembly will be starting in five minutes and I for one can't be late!" With that he marched off again out of the room and headed off along the opposite corridor away from the grand staircase.

"Come on Pythagorus and Newton." said their uncle grinning as he ushered them out of the room. "You'll get plenty of time to explore later and as the headmaster said, we can't be late!"

They headed off again along the corridor into another large hall with yet another staircase leading this time both up and down. They just caught sight of Artimas' back and his coat tails as he disappeared down the stairs, as by now he was almost running! They quickly followed him down the stairs that lead left into a large room which was also a minstrel gallery which must have spanned the length of the corridor. This gallery was the assembly hall and it was full of row upon row of chairs upon which sat rows and rows of pupils.

On one side of the gallery was a line of large windows which reached from the floor to the ceiling and looked out through the water, towards the lights of the city. In the water they could see lots of moving shapes of various sizes and colours which they assumed were fish. The windows also looked down onto the main courtyard in which they had first arrived on Ellie's back but there was no sign of her now. It was an awesome sight. On the other wall hung four large tapestries with pictures of the spirits; fire, water, air and the earth. These, they later learnt, represented the school houses.

As Neptune ushered them down the central gangway towards the stage at the far end of the hall, the twins could see that the other children sitting down wore different colour clothes. Black at the back, followed by red, gold, silver, blue, green and then lastly turquoise, the same colour as their own clothes. At the end of one of the rows near the front were two empty spaces with their names engraved onto the back of one of the seats.

"Sit down here boys," whispered Neptune, "and I'll come and find you later." And with that he disappeared towards the stage and a moment later they spotted him sitting on one of the chairs at the side of the stage.

Seated on top of the stage were about 30 teachers. Some of them were wearing cloaks in a multitude of bright colours and a couple wore pointed hats. A lot of the men had goatee beards. Some of them looked quite nice but some of them looked terrifying! All in all they looked nothing like the teachers they were used to at their old school. In fact, Uncle Neptune looked almost normal in comparison to some of the teachers who were now studying the new pupils in front of them very intently.

When they had first arrived the room was filled with the sound of voices, all talking and laughing at once. However, when Artimas walked onto the stage, the room instantly fell silent as the pupils crammed themselves forward so that they could listen to every word he said.

"Good morning boys and girls," shouted Artimas as he smiled at them all. "I hope you all enjoyed your holidays but I'm sure you are all glad to be back."

"Good morning Artimas." they all chanted back.

"Welcome to the start of another new term and in fact a new school year. And, of course a big welcome to year 8 who are in turquoise as usual and who are joining us for the first time today." He smiled at the pupils in the front five rows as he said this.

"House meetings will start in 15 minutes. Year 8 pupils, please wait here whilst we establish who you are and which house you will be joining. Please have your invitations ready. All the rest of you can go now. AND QUIETLY PLEASE." he added as the pupils had begun to chatter amongst themselves again the second he had dismissed them.

Pythagorus and Newton waited nervously as Artimas and four of the other teachers including Neptune approached them and the rest of year 8. They remained standing on the stage whilst the other teachers all disappeared off.

"Now then," Artimas said "for those of you who have never been here before let me explain. There are four houses at this school which are based on the four elements of nature i.e. Water, Air, Earth and Fire." He pointed to the tapestries as he said this.

"These are your housemasters" he then said pointing in the direction of the teachers who were standing behind him.

"Professor Neptune is the housemaster of water, Professor Glebe is housemaster of earth, Professor Brimstone is housemaster of fire and lastly, Miss Zephyr is housemistress of air. They will be your guides and mentors during your time here at school including for magic!" he told them adding "and if you have any problems or queries they are here to help you."

"You will be allocated to a house dependent upon a mix of your personal horoscope, which comes from the position of the stars in the sky at the exact moment you were born, and your own personality traits." he explained. "I have your horoscopes and personality profiles here." With that he patted a large pile of papers on the desk beside him. "But we still need to understand your inner spirits before a final decision can be made."

"Right," he said in a determined manner and waving his staff at them, "let's get on with it." He picked up the top piece of paper which was obviously a list of the new pupils and called them up to the stage, one by one.

After he had collected and checked that their invitation cards were valid, each pupil was directed to a specific teacher. This teacher then closed their eyes and placed their hands directly above the pupil's head. A few seconds later and in the space between their hands and the pupil's head a silvery light appeared and they could just hear the sounds of music. When they were with Uncle Neptune, this light became tinged with a blue aura, with Professor Glebe it became greeny brown, with Professor Brimstone, red and with Miss Zephyr white.

Sometimes when the pupil approached the first teacher the aura was not tinged with any colour at all. In these cases they were directed to the other teachers one by one until a coloured aura appeared. For each pupil an aura only appeared once with one of the teachers and this teacher then became their housemaster / mistress.

At last Artimas called out Pythagorus and Newton's name. Pythagorus went first and after handing in his invitation card to Artimas, he was directed towards Uncle Neptune. As he walked past the other teachers he could feel a heat coming from their hands and a silvery glow started to appear around his head. When he reached Uncle Neptune however he felt the heat intensify, the glow became tinged with a blue aura and he heard the distant sound of music. Uncle Neptune was to be his housemaster and he felt very glad. Uncle Neptune winked at him as he moved away to join the other pupils in his house who were all standing whispering in one corner of the stage.

When Newton approached the teachers, he too felt the heat from their hands and the same silvery glow started to appear. Like Pythagorus, he was first directed towards Uncle Neptune but to his horror, no coloured aura appeared and he couldn't hear any music. Artimas then directed him towards the other three teachers but despite walking past all of them twice, no colour appeared and the room became silent as everyone watched him curiously.

Artimas beckoned him over saying. "You my child are obviously one of those rare children who are guided equally by the four elements of nature. Come here and let me examine you myself."

As Newton walked back towards Artimas' outstretched hands the silvery glow exploded to fill the space between them and an aura of a multitude of colours shot out dancing from the glow and seemed to surround them both. At the same time the air became filled with the sounds of beautiful music. The other teachers and pupils gasped in surprise as they had never seen anything quite so beautiful. All except Uncle Neptune, who smiled to himself knowingly!

"Exceptional!" spoke Artimas in a deep low voice. "Almost unheard of at your age." he added smiling down quizzically at Newton who was wondering what all the fuss was about as he couldn't really see the aura that surrounded them. "I see we will have to take special care of you."

Everyone else in the room were now shaking their heads in disbelief and smiling at him. Except of course Pythagorus, who was looking at him puzzled, as privately he had always thought his twin strange and couldn't understand why everyone else was so impressed. It was only a coloured light after all!

"For now," Artimas said thoughtfully. "I think it's best if you stay with your brother so you will also be in the House of water."

Pythagorus and Newton grinned at each other, both relieved that they were not to be separated as they had never been apart since the day they were born. Pythagorus also had this feeling that his brother was going to need his protection and he was glad they were to be in the same house.

The last few children were then picked for their houses and then finally, the assembly was over.

"You must all go now and join your houses," Artimas told them, smiling at them all "and I hope you will be very happy here. School starts properly tomorrow at 8.30 am sharp." and with that he turned on his heels and was gone.

"Right, let's go." said Uncle Neptune to the twins and his other new charges. There were eight of them altogether. "It's time for you to meet the rest of the members of your house and we will only have a short meeting now to allow you time to unpack your bags. We will then meet again after lunch for your first lesson where we will concentrate on teaching you how to breathe properly for long periods under the water."

If we have time" he added "I will also introduce you to your sea horses. Now follow me." he told them and with that he ushered them out of the assembly hall, along yet another long corridor towards a room filled with the sound of voices and laughter.

"Are you all right Newton?" asked Pythagorus nudging his brother gently as he now looked a little pale.

"Yes, I'm fine," replied Newton. "but my head hurts a little from Artimas's hands and I still feel very hot." he added stroking his head as he spoke "It was just such a weird feeling!"

"I know just what you mean." responded Pythagorus. "Thank goodness that's all over. I'm so pleased that Uncle Neptune is going to be our housemaster. Some of the other teachers looked so fierce. All except for Miss Zephyr," he added. "I think she looked quite nice."

"I agree," grinned Newton still rubbing his head, "this feels like it's going to be such fun! What do you think he meant by the sea horses?"

"I'm not sure," replied Pythagorus, "perhaps they are Goldie and Koi. You remember, the names on those harnesses we were given."

"I'm sure you are right!" grinned Newton again. "I can't wait".

The twins then entered the room behind their uncle which was full to the brim with the other pupils in their house, all talking at once. They stopped as soon as they saw Neptune enter the room, and began to greet him enthusiastically.

Chapter 5

As soon as they entered the room, the noise subsided. Neptune stood up on a stool and ran though his register of children to check who was missing (Alfred!) and evicted the two he had gained in error (Sarah and Alex) before introducing the twins and the other newcomers to the rest of the members of the house. They were Rupert and Archie from England, Sofia from Russia, Courtney and Bradley from America, and Francois from France. None of them, with the exception of the twins had met each other before.

The house meeting lasted for about an hour and they soon became very bored because Neptune spent most of the time reading out instructions, telling people their sets and briefing them on their timetables. Most of it they didn't understand - I mean who wants to study Hydro electronics, or learn how to decipher the runes?

And what on earth was channeling?

When the meeting was finally over, Neptune led the eight of them back to their rooms so that they could unpack. To their surprise it seemed that they were all to share the same sitting room. Rupert and Archie were to the left of them in room 102, Sofia and Courtney were opposite them in room 103, and Bradley and Francois were to the right of them in room 104. They still didn't understand how their rooms could all end up in the same sitting room, but by now they were starting to accept everything as being normal.

"I'll come and collect you at 12.30," Neptune told them looking at his watch, "which will give you an hour to unpack and settle in. I'll then take you to the dining room for lunch. At 2pm sharp you will have your first lesson, which is learning to breathe under water with Miss Brenda Rethless."

"As I mentioned before," he added as he started towards the door, "if there is time afterwards, I will take you to the stables to meet your seahorses, but it depends upon how quickly you all learn to breathe."

"See you later!" he said waving as he disappeared swiftly back along the corridor.

Pythagorus and Newton then began the tedious task of unpacking their suitcases, which in the end didn't take them as long as they had expected. They put their Octopus quills on their desks together with some spare paper. Already on the desks were two jam jars filled with water marked "Snails", which were obviously homes for their water snails. There was also a folder marked "Useful Information" containing all sorts of admin details about the school. The mobile shell phones went beside their beds, and they hid the daggers under their mattresses.

Pythagorus had brought along some posters of his favourite all girl pop group and of a singer he secretly fancied and who used to be married to one of his football heroes. This poster he stuck up on the ceiling above his head. He had also brought along a poster of Manchester United who were his favourite football team. However, he wasn't sure how he was going to follow them, as when he had switched on his radio he couldn't find any radio stations!

Newton in the meantime had put some pictures of their parents and Silky their cat on the table in between their beds. He was the dreamer of the two and his posters were of the sky or of oceans full of dolphins, or of swirling images in a multitude of colours. As he placed them on the walls all around the room it started to feel like home!

When they had finished, they wandered into the sitting room and helped themselves to a couple of cold drinks they found in the fridge. They then flopped down onto one of the sofas and began to chat with Newton glancing at the folder they had found in their room as they talked.

"I'm looking forward to this afternoon," exclaimed Pythagorus excitedly. "I can't wait to learn how to breathe properly in the water so that we can start to explore. Do you think we will be allowed to visit the city?"

"I'm not sure," answered Newton, "there is a note in the folder which says that we are only allowed out of the school on Saturdays and Sunday afternoons. It says that Year 8 pupils have to be escorted by an older pupil so perhaps we can go then. I think we will have to ask Uncle Neptune for his help." he added.

"That won't be a problem." responded Rupert who had just come into the room followed closely behind by Archie. "My sister Verity is in year 12 and she can take us out whenever we want. It's not that interesting." he added nonchalantly.

"Have you been here before then?" asked Pythagorus, sounding impressed.

"Oh yes." replied Rupert flopping down next to him on the sofa. "I've already been here three times for speech day. I tell you it's not that exciting." he added almost yawning as he spoke.

"I don't believe you." responded Archie enthusiastically, "I can't wait. I've heard there are all sorts of machines and pieces of equipment like those shell phones we were given. I want to learn all about them." He too then flopped into a chair.

"I agree with Rupert." added Sofia haughtily as she walked into the room. She had spent the last twenty minutes brushing her hair and checking her lipstick. A strong smell of perfume wafted through the air as she walked past them to help herself to a cold drink. "Roll on the end of term when we can go home and I can see all my proper friends again. This is going to be so boring." She finished with a yawn of boredom.

"Has any one looked at their magic books yet?" asked Courtney studying them all intently one by one as she joined them in the room. "The book on "Hand rearing and training seahorses" looks absolutely fascinating. I can't believe we are not going to learn how to make Glycon until next year! And do you know what Quintessence is?"

"Don't you know how to make Glycon yet?" sneered Rupert.

"Well we don't." responded Pythagorus and Newton together. It was amazing how often they both spoke the same things at the same time.

"And we don't have any books at all yet." added Pythagorus.

"Nor do I." said Bradley as he jumped into the room to join them on one of the other sofas. Bradley seemed to be bursting with energy, like a young colt desperate to be free of his reins.

"Does anyone know which days we have sport? I hope we won't be indoors all day every day or I shall die!" he added with a deep sigh.

"No." they all responded.

Francois finally wandered into the room and also joined them on the sofas, which by now were almost full! "Well!"

he said, looking them all up and down, one by one. "Let's just hope we all get on!"

"I'm sure we will." responded Newton getting up as he was starting to feel a bit squashed! He began to wander around the room examining all the pictures on the walls as he continued to listen to the others' conversation.

"What are we going to call ourselves?" asked Rupert. All of the study groups in the school have a special name to distinguish themselves from the other study rooms."

"How about The Champions?" suggested Bradley?

"No, that's no good." replied Rupert. "There's a group in year 10 with that name already."

"How about The Connoisseurs?" suggested Francois?

The others gave him a strange look before Sophie said, "I don't think so. That just sounds awful."

"As Newton and I are twins, and there are 8 of us how about the Octets?" suggested Pythagorus sensing an argument brewing.

Laughing, they all agreed that it was a great name and very appropriate. They then began to talk amongst themselves, questioning each other as to where they came from and what they knew about the school. It turned out that only Rupert had been to the school before, but Sofia had heard all about it from some family friends back in Russia.

Whilst they were all talking, Newton, who was still listening to all of their conversations continued to explore the room. Next to one of the pictures of a dolphin by a door and just below the ceiling he discovered two sets of switches, which he presumed were for the lights. When he pushed the first set, they switched on the main light above their heads and the two lamps on the tables by the sofas.

When he pressed the second set however, which were partly hidden by the dolphin picture, no lights came on. Instead there was a loud grinding noise, similar to the noise they had experienced in the chamber at the entrance to the school. At the same time, the floor beneath them began to move away from the centre of the room towards the walls, slowly at first and then quickening as a large hole opened up beneath their feet.

In the end the floor moved so quickly, Newton had to jump up onto a sofa in order to stop himself from being squashed up against the wall and almost landed on top of Sofia who by now was on the verge of screaming. They all gasped in shock as the floor beneath them disappeared.

Chapter 6

By the time the sofas and tables had reached the walls, about half of the floor had gone and they found themselves looking down into the clear water beneath them and directly towards the ocean bed.

They didn't realise it at the time but the floor was covering a large circular layer of Glycon.

"What an earth did you do Newton? "gasped Rupert.

As he spoke they all peered down into the water where a few fish could be seen in the distance. Before Newton could reply and just as they were getting used to the eerie light, suddenly a brown nose and a pair of piercing yellow eyes appeared at one of the edges of the circle. The eyes stared at them, seeming to study them all for a few seconds before they heard a soft neighing noise and the eyes moved forward to reveal a sea horse swimming in the water below them. Another one immediately joined him and the pair swam around underneath the glass looking up at them. They both seemed to be trying to communicate with them as they continued to neigh, flicking their tails and sometimes nudging the floor with their noses in greeting.

They were both light brown with rounded silvery tails. A line of dark brown triangles edged down their backs, right down to the tips of their tails. Half way down their backs were two, small, transparent wings, which fluttered all the time they swam in the water sending spiraling rays of bubbles in their wake. As they moved about, their wings also reflected back the light from the room into the water with streaks of light blazing through the water full of all the colours of the rainbow. They were about eight feet long, if you included their curly tails. On the top of their heads they each had a crown of shiny silvery hair, which stuck up from their heads, punk style! Their eyes were as bright as the mid-day sun.

The only difference between them was that one of them had a gold smudge on the tip of his nose, and the other had a red smudge on his forehead. They both looked like they were smiling.

"Wow!" said Newton as he jumped down off the sofa and without thinking crawled onto the Glycon floor so that he could be closer to them. He put out his hand on top of the floor and one of the sea horses, the one with the gold patch, came up to him and tried to nuzzle his hand. At this they all laughed and the sea horse seemed to become quite huffed as he flicked his tail and turned his back on them. It was as if he wanted to be stroked and was cross that he couldn't get nearer to them!

"Aren't they beautiful?" sighed Courtney as she and Pythagorus joined Newton on the floor, their hands also stretched out in greeting.

"I can't wait to ride on one of them," exclaimed Bradley excitedly. "I hope they are as easy to ride as normal horses. Do you think we'll get a chance today?" he added.

Even Rupert looked impressed as they watched them gliding around in the water below them. Then a few minutes later, and with another flick of their tails they were gone, and the water seemed very empty and dark without them.

"We'd better close up the floor as it's nearly lunch time." said Archie a few minutes later jumping up and playing with the switches before anyone else could stop him. He flicked the switches a couple of times making the floor slide backwards and forwards and knocking everyone off the sofas before finally letting it close up again. As the clock on the wall chimed on the half hour above Francois' head, the sofas and table settled back into their original positions and Neptune came striding back into the room. Luckily for them there was no sign of the recent events.

"Great." he said smiling at them all. "You all look ready for lunch." And with that he turned on his heels and led them out of the sitting room and back along the corridor towards the dining room.

"Settling in?" he asked them as they marched along the corridor.

"Yes thanks." They all chimed in unison as they tried to keep up with him.

As they walked along the corridor Newton whispered to Pythagorus "Do you think that sea horse with the gold patch is Goldie and the other one Koi?"

"Yes I think so." replied Pythagorus.

The dining room was similar to the Great Assembly Hall but went along beneath the opposite corridor. It was filled with round tables and chairs and the "Octets" quickly found themselves a table to sit at. In the middle of each table were some dishes sitting on top of hot plates filled to the brim with piping hot food. The smell was delicious. Today, it was fish soup, followed by shepherd's pie and a fruit trifle for desert. There were large silver servers for them to help themselves. Pythagorus and Newton were surprised at how hungry they suddenly felt and quickly demolished their lunch. It did however all taste a bit fishy, and they now understood why their Uncle Neptune liked their mothers' cooking so much.

Yet again the room was filled with the sound of voices and laughter. The teachers were scattered around the room and some of them were even eating at the same tables as the pupils. As they ate, some dinner ladies wandered

43

around the room bringing drinks of water and orange juice and extra bread. For the first time that day, they actually felt like they were at school. But a very posh school!

Lunch was soon over, and Uncle Neptune again led them out of the dining room along another long corridor, but this time towards a huge oak door.

Waiting impatiently for them in front of the Great Oak door, was their swimming teacher Miss Brenda Rethless. She was dressed in a turquoise bathing robe but it didn't quite fit properly and they could see that she was wearing an orange bathing suit underneath it. In one of her hands was a purple swimming cap and her blonde hair was tied up in pigtails. She was very large. In fact she was so plump; she could only just tie up her bathrobe around her tummy! She looked so comical, that Archie began to snigger, but quickly stopped under the glare of Uncle Neptune's eyes.

"Good afternoon Brenda." said Uncle Neptune. "These are your year 8 pupils" and he introduced them one by one. They all said hello nervously because she also looked quite scary. She boomed a greeting to them in a large deep voice.

"I will come and collect them all at 4pm, if you will have finished with them by then as I'd like to introduce them to their seahorses before teatime. Call me if there is a problem." he said to Miss Rethless. "Behave yourselves!" he added sternly to the Octets, and then he was gone.

"Come along now and follow me." said Miss Rethless, as she waddled away towards a smaller door nearby, which opened, into a large changing room filled with cubicles. "Boys, you go to the left and girls you go to the right. You will find a selection of swimming costumes, trunks and caps in the cubicles, together with some towels. Hurry up and change so that we can begin our lesson." she instructed them as she walked away.

They all entered into one of the cubicles and, as she had told them, there was a large selection of swimming costumes in a variety of sizes waiting for them. It took a little time for Archie and Newton to find some trunks that didn't immediately fall down around their legs, but Pythagorus had no problem. Sofia couldn't find a swimming costume that was fashionable enough for her, but eventually found one that fitted! All the time they were changing, they could hear Miss Rethless huffing and puffing as she shouted at them to hurry up.

She was very impatient!

Finally, and giggling at each other, they were ready and they left their cubicles to meet Miss Rethless in the middle of the room. She looked them up and down and appeared satisfied with their appearance. She then led them out through the back of the changing room on to a wide balcony.

The balcony was situated at the end of a vast room which was twice the height of the changing room and probably as long as the Great Assembly Hall. It was difficult to tell its exact size. There were more large windows, which stretched from the floor to the ceiling all along one of the walls. Somehow again, they were looking out over the central courtyard, but they were obviously positioned on the other side of the courtyard as they could now see the main entrance door with the clock tower above. On the opposite wall, which was painted a basic colour of pale blue, was a vivid tableau portraying whales and dolphins playing in an ocean. It was a beautiful and rather overwhelming sight.

In the centre of the room, was a huge glass, or possibly a Glycon tank, which was filled to the brim with crystal clear water. It was so large; there wasn't the space for anything else to fit into the room but it looked like you could just

45

about walk around it. Steps from the balcony led straight down into the water. It was an amazing sight!

"Right then" said Miss Rethless as she put on her purple swimming cap and matching goggles, which she brought out of one of her pockets. She then took off her bathing robe to reveal a large bust, which must have been larger than the complete width of Archie's chest: and a stomach to match! Her orange swimming costume looked so stretched; you had the impression it was going to tear itself apart at any moment.

She was an amazing and colourful sight to behold, and even Bradley, athletic as he was, shrank back in awe.

"You are now going to learn how to breathe properly under water,." she began. "The secret is to close your mouths tight and breathe in the water through your nostrils. Inside the lining of your noses, you each have a special pair of filters, which prevents the water from entering into your body. The filters also extract the oxygen from the water thus enabling you to breathe under water. They act like a door, which is either left open, as now, or closed when you are under water. These filters are inherited from your ancestors and are one of the things that make you different from normal human beings." she explained quickly.

"The difficult part," she continued, "is switching the filters in place i.e. closed as you enter the water and then open again when you leave the water. You just need to learn to twitch your nose so that you can open and close them at will. It's just a question of instinct in the same way that you lift your arms or move your legs to walk. If you remember when you learnt how to ride a bike, all it took was practise, but once you learnt you never forgot." At this she smiled at them all.

Courtney looked very worried at this point, because if there was one thing she had never been able to master, it was riding a bike. She prayed that swimming would not be that difficult!

"On the floor over there," Miss Rethless added, pointing to a box in the corner of the balcony, "are some small tanks of oxygen and some masks, which you will need to put on. They are for when you initially enter the water, and thereafter for emergencies only. As soon as you've put them on," she finished, "we'll begin our first lesson."

Once they were ready, which only took a couple of minutes, they nervously approached the steps leading off the balcony and into the tank. "Follow me." shouted Miss Rethless enthusiastically in a loud voice, and without another word she jumped off the top balcony step straight into the water and immediately disappeared from view.

As she jumped in, she held her nose tight between two fingers of one hand, and held the other hand high in the air above her head. She looked very funny! When she jumped in she created such a huge splash that they were all instantly drenched from head to toe.

"She reminds me of a hippo jumping into the water like that!" whispered Newton to Pythagorus. But they all heard him and started to laugh.

In fact they were all laughing so much, they didn't see their teacher emerge from the water, and so she made them all jump out of their skins when she shouted at them again to hurry up!

One by one, they jumped in the water. As you would have expected, Bradley dived in first with a perfect dive, closely followed by the twins. Archie was second to last as he was not a good swimmer, whilst Sofia was last as she was worried about ruining her hair.

Sophia wished she had managed to find a swimming cap that fitted nicely but Miss Rethless hadn't given them enough time for her to look properly, and the sight of Francois's tan had distracted her. She hated her teacher so much at that moment as she reluctantly jumped in.

Once under the water Miss Rethless led them to the centre of the tank where they found some tables and chairs and they all sat down. There was even a houseplant on one of the tables but no pens or paper. To one side was a large blackboard upon which she began to write instructions with a special chalk on how to twitch their noses and switch open and close their filters, but it was a bit difficult to hear her properly under water. Their first lesson had begun in earnest!

After a few attempts at swimming and breathing without the oxygen tanks, both Pythagorus and Newton started to feel a sensation deep inside their noses and when they concentrated hard, they could feel something move. Depending upon which position these filters were in their noses, they could either breathe quite happily under the water or they couldn't. To their delight, within about half an hour, the masks and oxygen tanks were superfluous to them, as they had mastered the art of moving their filters. All the years of practising swimming under water in the cove had obviously helped them.

Once they had got to this stage, Miss Rethless sent them away with a wave of her hands so that she could concentrate on the others and they were able to explore the rest of the tank. In one corner, they found some footballs, and at the far end they found some goalposts so they began to kick the ball around and play football. It was however more difficult than it sounds, as every time they kicked the football it floated up towards the surface and not towards the goalposts, so they had to keep jumping up in the water to catch it. It was still quite fun.

After a few minutes, Bradley joined them, but it was some time before any of the others arrived. Courtney had eventually found that it wasn't as difficult as she had feared, and Archie initially had a problem with swimming and breathing at the same time but was soon sorted. Sofia however, just couldn't master her filter system and was still using her oxygen tank and mask by the end of the two-hour session. She was not amused, and Newton felt quite sorry for her and vowed to help her next time.

Miss Rethless however seemed quite happy with the success of the session and even smiled at them all when they finally got out of the water. Sadly, she looked even more frightening when she smiled as all they could see were her teeth!

Chapter 7

It felt cold when they came out of the water and they all started to shiver, so Miss Rethless hurried them back into the changing rooms to get dressed. When they eventually came back out of their cubicles, they found her gossiping with Uncle Neptune and smiling up at him in a very strange way and for some reason she kept blinking quickly as she looked at him. They were sipping two, hot, steaming cups of hot chocolate.

"Ugh." said Pythagorus and Neptune together when they first saw them talking but their uncle gave them both a grateful look when they arrived to interrupt the conversation. They helped themselves to a cup of steaming hot chocolate from the drinks machine. It was sweet and delicious and thankfully didn't taste at all fishy! The others soon joined them, although Sofia took a bit longer as she had to tidy up her hair first. Uncle Neptune was very pleased with the reports of their progress and kindly told Sofia not to worry. He was sure she would get the hang of it next time.

Uncle Neptune then agreed that they had changed quickly, and so, as promised, they had just about enough time to visit the seahorses in the stables, provided they didn't linger too long over their drinks. They all drank them up quickly, narrowly avoiding burning their mouths.

"I'm ready now Uncle, please can we go?" Newton asked excitedly, putting down his empty mug.

"Alright then Newton," Uncle Neptune said smiling, "but as I said we only have about half an hour, so you will need to walk fast. Come on hurry up and follow me."

He led them out of the cloakroom and back towards the Great Oak Door. He punched in some numbers on the keypad lock on the door, and a green light scanned his eyes and face before the lock on the door clanked back. They were surprised at the sophistication of the lock as the door looked so old! Uncle Neptune was then able to open the door but it was very heavy and he had to push it quite hard.

When he finally opened the door, they found themselves looking into a small courtyard. In the centre and in front of them was a clear tunnel, made of Glycon, leading away from the door, and through the water towards the stables which were about 500 metres away on the other side of the courtyard. They could all sense all sorts of interesting things awaiting them here, and they were very excited!

Uncle Neptune immediately strode off through the tunnel towards the stables without a backward glance with the Octets having to almost run to keep up with him. The tunnel was filled with air, so they had no problems breathing as they hurried along. As they walked along the tunnel however, they could feel the floor moving under their feet with every step. It seemed that even the floor was made of Glycon and they seemed to bounce along it rather than walk.

As they got further into the tunnel, the floor suddenly seemed to register the effect of so much weight on it and the whole tunnel began to gradually sway in the water, moving gently up and down creating ripples of water and bubbles in its wake. It was an odd but pleasant sensation but it made trying to walk rather difficult! It was like trying to walk in a bouncy castle.

The bubbles and the movement in the water soon attracted the attention of the seahorses in the stables in front of them and their heads began to appear above the stable doors, one by one. They were all watching them approach with the most curious looks on their faces. The Octets were so fascinated by the sight of the seahorses ahead of them, that they didn't even notice the shoal of yellow and blue fish, which had arrived in the courtyard and were now swimming along beside them. The fish seemed as equally curious about the children in the tunnel as the children were about the seahorses.

By the time they arrived at the entrance door to the stables, which only took about five minutes, all of the seahorses were now looking over their stable doors watching them. Now that they were closer, they could see that they all had different faces. Some had different coloured markings, spots or stripes. Some had a large patch over one eye, whilst others looked like they had on a face mask. All of them looked like they were studying the children intently and they began to smile when they finally arrived – or so it seemed.

When the tunnel reached the stable entrance it split into two smaller tunnels. One led directly into the stables through a glass door whilst the other went along the front of the stables towards a door at the other end. The tunnel was built in the shape of a T and the same keypad lock that they had seen on the Great Oak Door locked each door.

"Is that Goldie and Koi!" exclaimed Pythagorus as he pointed excitedly to the two seahorses they had seen earlier from their sitting room. They were now in a stable at the far right end of the stables. Newton nodded his head in agreement.

"That's right!" responded Uncle Neptune somewhat startled. "How did you know that?"

"Oh, just guesswork." replied Newton as he looked away from his uncle very sheepishly. His uncle looked at him very suspiciously, but decided not to say anything.

"Well you are both right." he added walking towards the seahorses and pointing to them. "These are to be your seahorses. They have all been chosen especially for each of you and hopefully, they will be your friends for the next seven years whilst you are here at the school."

"You will be expected to look after them at all times," he continued "but that doesn't include feeding them or cleaning out the stables as we hire stable boys to deal with that. They will carry you to the city when you are allowed to leave the school premises, but more importantly, you will ride them in the seahorse races later this year. This school, and especially our house, has a strong tradition of seahorse racing, and hopefully there will be a House or even a School champion amongst you."

He looked at them all thoughtfully as he said this.

"The trials will begin at the end of next week to give you all an opportunity to learn how to ride them first. Don't worry," he added. "it won't take you long to learn,"

"Newton, let me introduce you to your seahorse first." he said, leading him towards the seahorse with the gold patch on one side of his face. "As you guessed, this is your seahorse Goldie. He is descended from the first seahorses kept by the royal family of Atlantis, some 5000 years ago. Talk to him and make him your friend and he will serve you well." he finished.

"Just remember at all times, "Uncle Neptune continued, "that he is a wild creature, free to go wherever he pleases, and that he has chosen to spend his time with you. If you treat him badly," he warned," he will leave you." Uncle Neptune looked quite severely at them as he told them this. "But treat him with love and respect and he will be your best friend." he finished.

Uncle Neptune then nodded his head towards Goldie, who bowed his head in return. Newton copied him and also bowed his head towards Goldie, and to his delight, Goldie responded and nodded his head again towards him.

Newton stayed to talk to his new friend, placing his hand on the tunnel wall between them. He longed to be able to stroke him but he couldn't yet. Uncle Neptune meanwhile moved away and began to introduce Pythagorus to his seahorse, Koi.

Koi had a bright red circle on his head between his ears; hence he had been named after the Japanese Koi carp, which is the most treasured fish of Japan. He was also of royal blood and he seemed to be excited at meeting Pythagorus as he started to jump up and down in the water creating a stream of bubbles around him. Pythagorus in turn was pleased at how powerful and strong he looked. Much stronger than Goldie, he thought to himself. To him, Goldie looked highbred but too gentle to be a champion.

Neptune then introduced the other children to their seahorses, none of whom however were of royal blood. Bradley's seahorse was called Pegasus. Unusually, he was jet black rather than brown with a white face and mane. He also looked very strong and muscular and Bradley was very pleased.

D'Artangan was to belong to Sofia. He was dark brown with a jet-black mane and he looked very proud with his head held up high. Lancelot was to belong to Francois and he had a white diamond on the front of face, which covered his nose. He also looked very noble.

Courtney's seahorse was called Hercules. He had a white patch over one eye, and looked very strong and sturdy. Not at all aristocratic, but Courtney was very happy with him. Quiver, who was hiding behind his stable door, was to belong to Archie. He had white tips on the ends of his mane which made it look like it had been dipped in paint. He was a little nervous as he was only a young seahorse but he seemed to grow in confidence when he met Archie. They were going to make a great pair!

Finally, Rupert was introduced to his seahorse, Prince. He was also dark brown, with white smudges all over his face. They both seemed very disinterested in the whole proceedings, but perked up a little when they met each other.

Uncle Neptune was very pleased with their reactions. He and Jock had obviously chosen well.

The Octets spent about ten minutes talking to their own seahorses, and then spent some more time looking at each other's seahorses and comparing notes. They all decided that they were very happy with the seahorses that had been picked for them. Even Rupert was pleased! Bradley was desperate to ride Pegasus straight away, but knew that he had to wait.

"Time's up, "said Uncle Neptune looking at his watch "or we will be late for tea. Don't worry you will meet them again when you have your first riding lessons tomorrow with Jock Hunter."

"Can't we stay a bit longer?" asked Bradley.

"Please, please." begged Courtney smiling at him sweetly.

"Yes please Uncle Neptune." pleaded Pythagorus as his Uncle shook his head at them.

"Just five more minutes?" added Newton, hopefully.

"I'm sorry," responded Uncle Neptune, "but as I have already told you, Artimas is a stickler for time and today is the first day of term. Anyway, it's also feeding time for the seahorses. Look, there's Peter the stable boy now." He pointed to the corner of the stables where they could see a teenage lad had just arrived arriving carrying two large buckets of food. Suddenly all the seahorses now seemed more interested in what he was carrying than looking at the Octets.

So reluctantly, they followed Uncle Neptune back along the tunnel, through the Great Oak Door and on towards the dining room. All the way they were talking and laughing amongst themselves excitedly.

Dinner was roast beef and potatoes followed by ice cream. Pythagorus and Newton demolished their food, but strangely when they had finished they could again only taste fish afterwards! After dinner, Uncle Neptune led them back to their study rooms. By now, they were all starting to feel very tired and they were much quieter - It had been a very long but exciting day.

"Don't forget to phone home before you go to sleep, and I will see you all for a tutor period first thing tomorrow morning." he told them as they re-entered their study rooms. "You should find a copy of your timetables on your desks. Study them well as I'll be expecting you to have learnt them by the time I see you all tomorrow morning. Breakfast is at 7.30am so don't forget to set your alarms. Goodnight and sleep well." And with that he was gone.

After they had talked to the others for a while, Pythagorus and Newton went into their room to telephone their mum and dad on their new mobile shell phones. They felt a bit homesick when they first heard Katie's voice, but by the time they had told her all about their first day, this was soon forgotten.

It was very easy to use the phones. All you had to do was pick them up and say the name of the person you wanted to talk to. The next thing you knew, you were speaking to that person on the phone. It was very clever. They were tempted to phone Harry and Billy but they decided against it as they were so excited; they might say something they shouldn't! They decided they would write to them instead but they were just too tired to start writing any letters so they would have to wait to another day.

They both slept very soundly that night, their dreams full of seahorse races, of Ellie and thoughts of all of the adventures they were going to have in this new land.

Chapter 8

The following morning, after a breakfast of toast and cereal, Pythagorus and Newton headed off to their house common room for an early house meeting. The others soon joined them. Their common room was actually two rooms with the middle wall knocked out. It had long windows similar to those in the dining room but it faced the opposite way and overlooked the city instead. The room was filled with tables and comfy chairs scattered at random around the room. There was a drinks machine in one corner, whilst in another was a silver statue of a dolphin. One wall of the room was covered from floor to ceiling with a bookcase full of books on ocean life and animals and other subjects which they had never heard of. They didn't have time to look at them, but Pythagorus and Courtney were both looking forward to investigating them later.

The best part of the room however, was the ceiling, which was painted Italian style with a mural of people and angels in the centre, surrounded by more dolphins, whales, seahorses and other sea creatures. The edges of the painting were a turquoise blue, with pinks and greens in the centre. Overall, it was vibrant with colour and movement and it was obvious that the ceiling depicted the element of their house, which was water. Uncle Neptune later told them that he was very proud of this mural, which had been painted by their mum, Katie, when she was at the school. The twins in turn felt very proud.

Looking through the windows, they were surprised to see that the school was in fact on top of a hill looking down over the city. They could see a line of stones leading away from the school, which must have been a path or road when the school was originally above the water. At the bottom of the hill they could see houses and buildings that looked like shops

. In the distance, they could see a church and what looked like another chateau. There were many buildings which they could not identify, but certainly looked interesting. In the far distance they could just about make out a wall which seemed to circle the city, and beyond was just land and water that seemed to stretch out as far as the eye could see. In the old days, it was probably fields. Everywhere they looked they could make out twinkling yellow lights and they were both desperate to explore.

They quickly ran through their timetables with Uncle Neptune and they were surprised to see how many normal lessons they still had - Latin, French, English and Chemistry, as well as lessons in "The History of Oceana", Seahorse riding, the study of Dolphins and Marine life (Uncle Neptune's subject), and of course the study of Ancient Magic. Not surprisingly, this was Artimas', the headmasters' subject. They had very busy days, which started at eight thirty in the morning and finished at five every night.

 The bad news was that on top of this they had an hour's homework every day!

After dinner, there were some clubs they could join for an hour such as chess, drama or lace making (!). Saturday was sports day and Sunday was their rest day. They were pleased to see that church on Sunday mornings was not compulsory.

Once Uncle Neptune had finished, they headed off to their first lesson, which was English. They were to study "A Midsummers' Night's Dream" by someone called William Shakespeare. They quite enjoyed reading out the individual parts. Pythagorus played Oberon, King of the fairies, whilst Newton played a mischievous spirit called Puck. There was some sniggering when Rupert was given the part of Bottom a foolish actor!

Next came Latin, followed by Maths (Trigonometry) and then a short break. They all headed back to their house common room, where they found some fresh fruit and cold drinks laid out on a table. They later learnt that Ellie and some of her friends transported the fruit, together with letters from home down from the surface every day. There were some sixth formers sitting on tables and chairs chatting away. The sixth formers stared at them when they first entered the room and then ignored them. All except for one, Eugene their house captain, who got up and greeted them all when they came in the room.

There's some letters over there that have arrived from the surface," he said pointing to a pile of post on a table. "You'd better check to see if there are any for you."

Pythagorus and Newton looked through the letters but there were none for them. The only one of the Octets to receive a letter was Sofia, and she received two! I'm afraid to say that she did gloat about this for a while.

"We get the post at first break every day." explained Eugene smiling at them. He then turned away and continued his conversation with his friends.

Pythagorus helped himself to a coke, whilst Newton had a lemonade. They then joined Rupert and the others who were all chatting in the corner on a sofa.

"What did you think of Latin this morning?" asked Archie excitedly. "I'm not sure if I am going to remember everything he said, but doesn't it sound strange."

"Haven't you learnt Latin before?" sneered Rupert, "It's easy."

Pythagorus and Newton quietly decided that Rupert should be less condescending, and if he didn't stop soon, they would tell him so! They were pleased that they weren't in the same set as him for some subjects. Despite him being six months older, he was in the bottom set for both maths and french!

"I can't wait for this afternoon." added Bradley excitedly. The thought of riding the seahorses was almost too much to bear.

Courtney was complaining bitterly over the fact that they only had three magic lessons a week; whilst Sofia and Rupert were complaining that they had to attend any of the lessons at all! Sofia was trying to read out her letters from home to them, but the others were completely ignoring her. Francois was lost in thought admiring the ceiling and wondering whether he would ever be able to paint such a beautiful picture.

Break was soon over and they continued on with their lessons.

Their next lesson was music with Miss Clang who was quite an extraordinary person. She was very thin and tall, almost like a beanpole. She had large feet, very long fingers with even longer nails, and a long pointed nose. Her hair was black and straight but stuck up at awkward angles from her head as if it hadn't been brushed for years. She was dressed in black from head to toe and she looked like a cross between a scarecrow and a witch, but she looked comical rather than frightening.

As she walked past them, they could smell Witch hazel.

Her first project was to teach them the school song. She sat at the piano and sang it to them in a high-pitched voice which didn't quite reach the high notes. They were all tempted to laugh but they didn't dare. It sounded a bit like the hymn "Early one morning..." but with different words. She soon instructed them to all join in and in the end it was quite fun. Afterwards, as they walked to the next lesson chattering together, they decided that she was quite nice and that it was by far the best lesson of the day.

They were soon in for a shock however, for as they entered the next room still chattering for history they were shouted at in a very sharp voice and told off for being both late and for talking. When they turned and looked at Mr Drill, their history teacher, he looked back at them with a very stern and harsh look. They quickly ran to their seats and sat down as he continued to glare at them.

Mr. Drill was the epitome of the teacher at school you most dread and least want to teach you. He was a tall, big man who looked like an ex sergeant major. He was neatly turned out in his pressed shirt and suit and smelt of cologne but you instinctively knew that you would be in big trouble if you arrived in his lesson looking a mess. He had a very harsh, booming voice that seemed to drone on for hours and hours.

He was very boring and very frightening and they all knew that history was to be their worst lesson. They weren't surprised when they later found out that he was to be their army cadet force teacher in year 10.

Afterwards came lunch, again in the dining hall. By now they had a collection of textbooks, and their quill pens had been put to good use. It was strange but they couldn't figure out the colour of the ink. Sometimes it was black, sometimes blue and sometimes even purple! Pythagorus and Newton were rather pleased when Uncle Neptune joined them at the table and they spent a long time telling him about their morning. He smiled at them affectionately as they chattered away, one finishing the sentence of the other as if they were one person rather than two.

The afternoon continued with a double lesson of art with Miss Zephyr, the housemistress of air. Her art room, which was also the "Air" common room, was located at the top of one of the towers. The room was in the shape of a fifty pence piece. It was a big, light and airy room with Glycon windows in the roof as well as the walls and the ceiling was painted pale blue with white, puffy clouds scattered here and there.

Hanging from the ceiling, were a number of bird mobiles of various shapes and sizes, which swung around in a gentle breeze created by the large fan hanging from the light in the centre of the ceiling. You had the feeling of being up amongst the clouds. All around the room were bookcases full of books on art and literature, gods and legends. Dotted on the tables were blue and white candles that smelt of vanilla.

Miss Zephyr they all agreed later was beautiful. She wore a bright blue cloak with more white clouds painted on it. The cloak floated and swirled as she walked around the desks, revealing a long white flowing dress underneath. She was slim with silver flowing hair and she always seemed a bit preoccupied, as if in another world. But they all agreed she was very kind to them as they sprayed paint on their paper with a paint spray, even when it went everywhere!□

Chapter 9

Then at last, the lesson they had all been waiting for arrived. Miss Zephyr had taken them back down to the Great Oak Door where Uncle Neptune was waiting for them. They had needed help finding their way around the building, despite the map they had been given as they were still very confused by the corridors, which all seemed to look the same and went in the same direction.

Neptune led them back along the glycon tunnel, which again rocked and swayed in the water as they bounced rather than walked along towards the stables. This time a shoal of orange fish swam past the tunnel, but again they didn't see them in their excitement to reach the stables. Their seahorses were peering over their stable doors waiting for them to arrive, but now they could see that they were wearing bridles over their heads.

"Today," Uncle Neptune explained as they walked along the tunnel, "you will be wearing your oxygen tanks and masks again. I know you all did very well yesterday, but we don't want any accidents this early on in the term! You have another swimming lesson tomorrow." he added smiling at them "So hopefully by this time next week, we can put the tanks away again until next year."

They all nodded their heads in agreement as they were getting more and excited as they approached the stables.

When they finally arrived at the stable door, Uncle Neptune pressed a couple of numbers on the keypad, the door opened and they entered the stables.

To their surprise they looked just like the sort of stables you can find scattered all over England and there was even a faint smell of horse in the air. There was straw strewn all over the floor and on two sides of the walls, and hanging on rows of pegs, were a collection of riding hats, crops, saddles and bridles. In a heap in one corner of the room was a pile of riding boots, whilst in another corner there was a pile of clothes. There were some pictures of seahorses and rosettes hanging on one of the walls which Uncle Neptune explained were of past champions.

On the far side of the room, was a table and some chairs where they found both Peter the stable lad and Jock Hunter having a heated discussion over one of the seahorses. Peter gave them a quizzical look when they arrived and then disappeared out of the door without saying a word to them. Newton instinctively decided that he didn't like the look of him – he looked a bit shifty. He mentioned this to Pythagorus when they had a moment alone later, but Pythagorus hadn't had the same feeling.

Jock Hunter was wearing a pair of jodhpurs, a red and white checked shirt and long, black riding boots. He was quite a big, muscular man, so his jodhpurs looked quite tight with his tummy hanging over the edge and his legs seemed to spill out of his boots. He was wearing a red, silk cravat tied around his neck. You half expected him to be wearing a cowboy hat, but for some reason he wasn't!

"Howdy guys," said Jock in a broad American accent studying them all very carefully. "I have a feeling that I am going to find a champion amongst you." His eyes rested on Pythagorus and Bradley as he said this. "Now then, who is who?" he asked.

The children introduced themselves one by one, and to their surprise he shook each one of their hands in greeting. Rupert told him that they were calling themselves the Octets and Jock grinned in approval. "Good name," he said "we won't be able to forget who you all are now." he added laughing.

"Right, come and put on some riding clothes as quick as you can so that we can go and meet your seahorses." Jock then told them pointing to the pile of clothes in front of them "I have some oxygen cylinders and masks here for you when you are ready."

Then turning to Neptune he added "Can you come and pick them up about five?" Neptune nodded his head in agreement and then headed back to the main school through the stable door.

The Octets were soon ready. They followed Jock out of the stable door and through into a vacuumed chamber similar to the one at the main entrance to the school. This time however, when Jock pressed a silver knob, the chamber filled with water and they only just had time to quickly put on their masks and switch on their oxygen tanks. He then opened up the outer door and led them towards the stable boxes, walking under the outer edge of the stable roof, which stuck out over the building to form a sheltered walkway.

This time Newton had no problem keeping himself on the ground and as they walked along the walkway they could hear the seahorses neighing, with voices that sounded like flutes as they walked towards them.

As soon as the seahorses saw them approach, they jumped or rather glided out of their stable boxes and flew through the water towards them, Quiver trailing nervously at the back. Sofia was a bit nervous when she saw them all hurtling towards them and hid behind Jock, peeping round his legs to watch. As if telepathic, each seahorse aimed towards his new owner, stopped just in time, and began to nuzzle them and gently head butt them in greeting. A wave of bubbles followed behind them.

Sofia decided that it was perhaps safe after all and stopped hiding.

Jock then helped them mount on to their seahorses at the same time showing them how to use the stirrups and the bridle. Bradley in his enthusiasm jumped up on to Pegasus too quickly and promptly went sailing straight over his back and fell in a crumpled heap on the floor. Although he was not amused, everyone else found it very funny!

Then, as they started to move off, Archie's seahorse, Quiver stopped suddenly, startled by a fish that swam past him and Archie went flying straight over his head and also landed in a heap on the floor, twisting his ankle in the process. He was however very brave, and after an apologetic nuzzle from Quiver he immediately climbed straight back onto his back.

Jock led them slowly around the stable courtyard, so that they could get used to the feel of the seahorses. It was very difficult to stay in the saddle because the seahorses didn't always glide slowly or stay in one direction. Most of the time they seemed to jump forwards, often at an angle, or they quickly spun around because they wanted to look at something behind them. Sometimes they even went sideways!

Within a few minutes they had all fallen off! Rupert managed to bang his head once when he fell, but none of them really hurt themselves. In fact they spent most of the time laughing at each other as one by one they fell off their seahorses and landed sprawled out on the floor.

By the end of the two-hour lesson, they had all managed to stay on their seahorses for about half an hour without falling off, but none of them had mastered the art of controlling either the direction or the speed of the seahorses. This was despite lots of pulling or yanking on the bridles or asking them very nicely! That was to be next week's lesson.

The seahorses seemed quite upset when they left them, but quickly cheered up when they saw Peter arrive with their dinner and started neighing to each other. They especially liked the sight and smell of the carrots he was carrying which were a rare treat as normally they were only given seaweed! They quickly returned to their stables to eat.

Very tired, bruised all over but excited and all talking at once despite their masks the octets walked back into the vacuumed chamber. Jock pressed another button, and just like before, the water immediately drained away and they were instantly dry. They were very pleased to see Uncle Neptune waiting for them in the warmth of the stables. Pythagorus and Newton dashed over to tell him how their first lesson had gone and the others piled in after them all talking at once.

The Octets quickly changed and were soon ready to go back to school. They followed Neptune back through the tunnel, still all talking at once and went straight to the dining room for their dinner. As they were all so tired, after dinner they headed back to their study rooms for a bath and an early night. As Pythagorus and Newton were very conscientious, they completed their homework first! They then telephoned their parents and told them excitedly about their first proper day of lessons. They now knew that they were really going to love this school but within a few minutes, they were both fast asleep, and practising riding their seahorses as they slept!

Chapter 10

The next morning, Pythagorus and Newton woke up bright and early. They were looking forward to today. Not only did they have another swimming lesson with Miss Rethless, but they also had their first lesson with Artimas. They couldn't wait to see what he was going to cover in his lessons. But first, there was a chemistry lesson for them to go to.

Professor Brimstone, the housemaster of fire and his laboratory assistant, Mr Magnihyde, taught chemistry, as well as all of the other science subjects. Professor Brimstone looked very normal, despite being a chemistry teacher, with a short crew cut hairstyle and a blue suit but there was a strong smell of sulphur whenever he walked past. He also had a very high pitched and squeaky voice when he talked, and he got very excited when they carried out their first experiment and his voice seemed to get higher and higher with each minute.

The first experiment was to heat a strip of magnesium over the flame of a Bunsen burner. When it gets to a certain temperature it burns with a bright white light, and is best viewed with the lights off. The Octets had never seen this before, and by the way Professor Brimstone was jumping up and down in excitement, you would think that it was also his first time!

In a funny way, they were quite relieved when the lesson was over – he was too exhausting to watch and listen to.

His laboratories were also very distracting to sit in. The walls were painted red and orange with red flames etched in black, painted flickering across the walls. There was also a distinct smell of smoldering embers although there was no sign of a fire anywhere.

His assistant, Mr Magnihyde seemed a bit creepy, especially to the girls who took an instant dislike to him. He was obviously a country and western music fan as he wore a denim shirt with rhinestones on it under his overall and a pair of cowboy boots, covered in tassels with a silver cap on the toes. Whenever you turned around, or looked up, he was there watching you, or so it seemed.

When Professor Brimstone first introduced them to him, he explained that it was also his first term and he had as much to learn about the school as they had. Mr Magnihyde didn't know anyone at the school, so they were told to be nice to him.

But they didn't like him at all, and they were so glad they were not in Professor Brimstone's house.

After another lesson of English, came a very welcome break. They then headed back down to the changing rooms and then the swimming tank where Miss Rethless was waiting impatiently for them. Today she was wearing a green swimming costume with a low cut back. Ugh! They quickly changed into their swimming costumes and headed onto the balcony where they were allowed to jump straight in. Only Courtney, to her utter embarrassment needed to use the oxygen tanks again.

Once under the water they joined Miss Rethless at the blackboard and sat down at the table and chairs. This time she proceeded to explain the rules of water hockey, Atlantian style. She used a piece of florescent pink waterproof chalk to draw diagrams on the blackboard of where players were positioned on the field, and to show various game strategies. Apparently, it was just like hockey but under water. The object of the game was still the same i.e. you had to score goals, but it was more like ice hockey where you were sometimes allowed physical contact with the other players.

To help them maneuver around and get up speed in the water, the games were played on water skates. She explained that they had to be very careful with the skates because if you went too fast you might not be able to stop and could end up hitting the edge of the tank. When you were playing outside, there was also the problem that you might skid, or trip and end up skating upwards in the water, rather than along the ground. Although you were allowed to dive and jump in the game, if you went above five feet or went out of the court, you were "grounded" and it was "time out" for five minutes.

There were three periods to the game each lasting 20 minutes with a 10 minutes break in between each period. As there was only eight in a team, the loss of a one member of the team was quite significant!

As you can imagine, the game went very fast!

Miss Rethless then pointed to the other end of the tank where they could just about make out a goal net, some sticks and other interesting looking objects. "Go and kit yourselves out," she told them "and see if you can skate around the tank without falling over whilst I see if I can sort out Courtney's breathing. Then I'll come and teach you how to play the game.".

The remaining Octets didn't take much persuading and they quickly swam off to investigate. They had thought they were just going to have another swimming lesson, but this was much more fun! Within a few minutes, they had all put on some skates and had found a hockey stick that they liked. They started to practise knocking the ball, which they later learned was called a puck, whilst trying to stay upright on the skates.

It had sounded very easy when Miss Rethless had first explained it to them, but trying to skate in the water and remain on the ground was not as easy as they had first thought. They all kept falling over and banging into each other. Newton, who did not have a good sense of balance at the best of times, kept finding himself either flat up against the wall of the tank, or up on the surface of the water. He loved it however when he dived back down! Even Sofia and Rupert thought it was good fun.

"How are you getting on Courtney?" asked Miss Rethless meanwhile at the other end of the tank, suddenly sounding surprisingly kind and smiling at her. "Can you feel your filters twitching yet?"

"Yes." replied Courtney hesitating, "But I can't seem to control them. It, it just seems to happen!" she added nervously.

"Right" replied Miss Rethless "this time I want you to start by winking at me. Now, concentrate very hard and close just one of your eyes and wink with the other. That's right," she told her, "now swap over and close the other eye and try again."

Courtney did as she was told and winked, first with one eye and then the other but it was not as easy as it sounds.

"Good." responded Miss Rethless encouragingly. "Now imagine that the filters in your nose are like your eyes, and try to close one side first and then the other but keep your eyes closed until you get the hang of it. Can you do that?" she asked.

Courtney closed her eyes and concentrated very hard, and to her delight, she found that with a little practice she could make each filter move by itself. She practiced a bit harder until suddenly she could move both filters together. She started to smile. Once she had done it a couple of times with her eyes open, Miss Rethless allowed her to take off her mask, and by the time half an hour had passed, she had mastered it completely and was able to join the others.

All the time she had been practising, she could hear them crashing and splashing around and muffled laughter. She was desperate to see what they were up to.

"Children, what an earth do you think you are doing?" shouted Miss Rethless as she finally caught sight of them rolling about and doing somersaults in a mock fight. They immediately stopped and all crashed to the ground in a heap. "Courtney, go and put on some skates and we will begin," she added, glaring at the others.

Miss Rethless then spent the next hour teaching them how to shoot goals with the hockey sticks. They were shorter than normal hockey sticks and had long rather than curved heads, and looked a lot like a golfing iron. The puck itself was made of a shiny, black, metal like substance and was so heavy that it didn't float in the water but just stayed close to the ground. It was also slightly warm to the touch. Because of the shape of the hockey stick it was quite difficult to control the puck or hit it in a straight line.

Once they had mastered how to control the puck, she then started to teach them some game tactics such as dive bombing your opponent and flicking the puck away from them without touching them. For most of the game, any form of body contact was banned and you would be grounded for five minutes if you touched another player so this was a skill that they would need to quickly master if they wanted to win. Playing the game on skates did not make this easy!

She then showed them how to block an opponent so as to stop them from getting an open shot at the goal. You could only do this within the shooting circle and this was the only time in the game that you were allowed any physical contact with your opponent. However, you could only steal the puck and avoid being grounded, if there was no body contact at all.

After a while, they soon found that they were all good at different aspects of the game.

To his surprise, Newton found that he was good at dive bombing and nipping in between his opponents and flicking the puck away from them without touching them. Pythagorus and Bradley were fast and strong with good hits, and made excellent midfielders. Rupert found he liked playing in defense – he didn't have to run around as much as some of the others, whilst Francois discovered a talent for shooting goals.

Sofia soon settled into centre midfield and Courtney felt quite at home in goal. I'm afraid to say her extra padding helped! Archie was not a strong swimmer but the skates gave him confidence and he was soon rushing around filling in the empty gaps on the field.

By sheer chance a natural water hockey team had evolved. Miss Rethless told them that Neptune was going to be so pleased when he found out, especially as there was a house tournament at the end of term. She also told Newton that he was a natural player and that being able to dive bomb your opponent successfully was normally something that took months if not years to master.

Tired, but very happy, the Octets finished their lesson and headed back to the cubicles to change. The smell of the steaming hot chocolate ensured that they quickly changed, but this time there was no Neptune waiting for them. They had to hurry and drink up their drinks very quickly as they were running late and if they didn't hurry up, they would miss their lunch. Miss Rethless had already rushed off and left them finishing their drinks so she could tell Neptune the good news.

Auditions for the junior choir followed immediately after lunch and of the eight, only Courtney and Rupert were picked to sing. The others were not too bothered however as anyone that did not sing was automatically in the drama club. Francois, who had acted in his previous school, instantly became the star pupil and was picked to take the lead as Romeo, in Romeo and Juliet. Despite all of her best efforts, Sofia failed to get the part of Juliet, but she did however get the part of the understudy. To his astonishment, and despite his shyness, Archie also picked up one of the lead parts, as Benvolio, Romeo's best friend. The other three just became members of the cast.

After the clubs came a geography lesson with Professor Glebe, housemaster of the earth house. His rooms were to be found deep in the basement of the school. Whereas Miss Zephyr's rooms were bright and airy, his rooms were dark and airless. There were no windows at all and the walls were all painted dark green or a muddy brown. There were no lights coming down from the ceiling, instead there were just a few wall lights. Some large church candles lit up the front and centre of the room sending shadows racing across the walls. The room was full of the smell of a strange musty incense and it was very gloomy and a little scary.

Professor Glebe himself also looked very drab and dreary. He was wearing a brown suit and spoke in a flat voice, never once looking up at them as he spoke. He just read from his lecture notes. The subject itself was also very boring – the formation of rocks! After such a busy morning, they found it difficult to stay awake and they spent all lesson yawning. At one point, Archie had to be prodded awake by Bradley. Annoyingly, Professor Glebe also gave them lots of homework.

"How on earth are we going to get through our geography lessons?" muttered Newton to Pythagorus as they left the lesson. They both promptly fell about laughing at his unintentional pun and soon found themselves feeling much better and wide-awake again.

Chapter 11

Immediately after geography they had to trek over to the other side of school to one of the other science laboratories, for their first lesson with Artimas, but they didn't carry out any experiments. Instead he spent the first lesson telling them more about the history of Oceana and their Atlantian ancestors. He also explained a little about the Glycon roof and tunnels – they were to learn how to make Glycon later on in one of their magic lessons.

Finally he explained how the schoolhouses, which were based on the four elements of nature, had developed. Some of the Octets had heard this story before, but they still found it very interesting.

"I inherited the position of headmaster from my father, who also inherited it from his father about 30 years ago, and he in turn inherited it from his father." Artimas began.

"Since the school started this position has been passed down the generations, mainly through the families of royal blood such as mine. The position of headmaster is one of the most important ones in our kingdom but the King and Queen obviously come first!" he added smiling.

"Before anyone can properly inherit the post," he continued, "they have to pass a number of tests including a detailed knowledge of Atlantian history, and a 100% pass rate in a special magic exam. They must also be a grandmaster and a member of the Atlantian Governing Council. Finally," he explained "their aura must be of the purest quality and include the whole spectrum of colours. This is only normally found in people with noble blood and even then the aura has to be developed over time to its full potential."

"Only when a person has passed all of these tests," he finished, "does he become a member of the Royal Privy Council and only then does he learn the most sacred of the magic secrets of our ancestors including how to help maintain the equilibrium of our world, which is, of course, of vital importance."

"The headmaster also inherits this magic staff." And at this point he patted the staff, which never left his side and the red ruby, which lay in the top of the staff in it's own cradle, seemed to come alive as a result of the sudden movement, and flickered as it caught the light. They had not noticed the ruby before but now it shone brightly, lighting up the room and making its presence felt. As they looked closer at the staff, they realised how old it must be from its wrinkled and worn appearance.

"What secrets did you learn?" asked Archie excitedly.

Artimas laughed. "I'm afraid I can't tell you that, otherwise they wouldn't be a secret anymore! But," he added seriously, "it is the secrecy that ensures that the magic powers of Oceana remain intact."

"Do you have a son or daughter who will learn all of your secrets one day?" asked Newton fascinated by what he had heard.

"No" said Artimas sadly, "and I'm too old to get married now, or to have children."
Rupert sniggered to himself.

"Instead," Artimas continued and ignoring him, "I'm looking for someone I can teach everything I know and pass on the Atlantian secrets. They need to be someone very special with an extraordinary talent for magic. They must also be very honest and kind and want to preserve the future of our kingdom at all costs, and of course," he added solemnly "they must be of noble birth."

As he finished speaking, his eyes rested thoughtfully on Newton who suddenly felt very hot under his gaze. Pythagorus, who spotted Artimas' look and felt his twins discomfort asked Artimas if the position had ever been held jointly. Artimas, sensing the reasons behind the question explained that it hadn't happened before, but that didn't mean to say that it couldn't happen in the future.

"Has there ever been a headmistress?" asked Courtney.

"No" responded Artimas kindly, "not yet."

"Who are the King and Queen?" asked Rupert who had always considered himself to be of noble birth.

"Our current King is Prince Henry and he is married to Princess Caroline." replied Artimas. "They live in a palace in the South of Oceana, but they often come and visit the school. Their eldest son, Prince Daniel is due to start at the school next year."

"Why isn't he called King Henry if he is the King," asked Sofia curiously.

"His father King Edward has retired, but by tradition Prince Henry will not be named King whilst his father is still alive," responded Artimas.

"That's a very beautiful stone," added Sofia, looking at Artimas' staff thoughtfully. "Is it a ruby? My mother would love to own it. Is it for sale?" she asked. "She has some earrings with the same colour rubies that would match it beautifully. How much do you think it is worth?"

The others gasped in astonishment at her cheek, and Artimas was momentarily taken aback.

"I'm afraid not," he replied coldly, drawing the staff towards him as he wrapped his arms around it protectively. "There is only one stone like this in the whole of the world. This stone is called the "Ruby of Life" and she is infused with the magic powers of our ancestors."

"According to legends," he started to explain stroking the ruby gently as he spoke. "If the ruby is taken out of Oceana and removed from the oceans, the minute it is touched by the oxygen and hydrogen in the earth's atmosphere it will disintegrate and our magic powers will be lost forever."

Looking at them all gravely he added "This power includes being able to create the magic ingredients within the powder which is sprinkled on the surface of glycon, as it is being made. If the ruby is destroyed and the magic is gone then the glycon will lose all of its strength, and will collapse under the weight of the ocean. Atlantica and all of its people would be destroyed forever."

"This staff" he continued, "will never leave my side. Only on my death will we be parted, and only then will it be passed it on to the next headmaster."

"Wow" whispered Pythagorus to Newton. "He looks very old. He must be at least ninety. Let's hope he finds a successor soon."

"I heard that comment Pythagorus" interrupted Artimas crossly.

How an earth had he heard them they thought, looking at each other in surprise as they were both sitting at the back of the room!

"I am only sixty five and I have no intention of dying just yet." Artimas told them sounding very disgruntled. "I intend to live for at least another fifty years." He added looking even more annoyed than before.

Luckily for both Pythagorus and Sofia, the bell rang for the end of the school day and Artimas strode off back to his room without a backward glance, clutching his staff in one hand and with his coat trailing behind him. He was clearly not amused.

"Newton, did you see how Artimas looked at you?" whispered Pythagorus as they wandered back to their room.

"No." responded Newton absentmindedly thinking about everything Artimas had told them. Pythagorus decided not to say anymore.

After dinner, and as it was Friday night, they joined the other pupils in their house for a general knowledge quiz night. It was the first time the whole house had been together socially, and it was good fun. Eugene, the house captain came and asked the twins how their first week had gone, and seemed very pleased when they told him about their first water hockey lesson. Rupert then introduced them to his sister Verity, who seemed much more down to earth than Rupert, and was very friendly. They also met Hugo, one of the prefects and also the House sports captain. To their delight, Eugene and Hugo both agreed to take the twins and the rest of the Octets out for a tour of the city on Sunday.

 They were all very excited at the prospect - even Rupert seemed chuffed!!

Chapter 12

Saturday, was the day they all played sports and it seemed to have come around very quickly. The whole school split into two and the first four years practised water hockey in the morning, and trained with their seahorses in the afternoon. The upper school, which was the top three years, were already skilled at water hockey and so had house matches all day. They started with the seahorse races in the morning and then finished with water hockey matches in the afternoon. As you can imagine, there just wasn't enough room in the water in the school grounds or the water tank for the whole school to play hockey at the same time!

It was amazing however, how many people you could fit in the tank. Miss Rethless had put up two nets as goals at the edges and a line of red balloons on streamers which were held down by pebbles to mark the outside of the court. All of the pupils got an opportunity to play in a game and the Octets were very proud when Francois scored a goal against one of the year 10 teams. They did however find it difficult to keep up with the pace of the game as the puck moved very quickly around the court.

After lunch, the Octets and the rest of their year were separated from the other years as they were not yet experienced enough to ride their seahorses outside of the stable yard. Instead, they were allowed to just ride around the yard and were told to practise staying on their seahorses. Jock Hunter kept his eye on them, but it was funny because it didn't seem quite so difficult for them this time, with only Archie having problems staying on his seahorse. Quiver kept stopping suddenly in a panic and time after time Archie would sail straight over his head into the water. Poor Archie!

Pythagorus and Newton in the meantime quickly learnt that somehow they could talk to Goldie and Koi, without speaking out loud. It was all in their thoughts, like a form of telepathy and Goldie and Koi always seemed to go where ever they were asked. They weren't sure if it was their imagination, but they could have sworn that they could hear the horses speak back to them. Koi even seemed to tell Newton off one time when they suddenly lurched to one side and nearly hit the tunnel!

When they discussed it with Bradley later they all agreed that being able to talk to their horses like this would be to their advantage in the races, as no one else would know which direction or angle they would take. Bradley didn't find talking to Pegasus quite as easy as the twins, but he was determined to practise.

 Of course what they didn't realise at this point was that all of the children in the school, some better than others, could talk to their seahorses in this way! They were all taught this in their magic lessons. Not all of them, however, could hear the horses talk back.

Whilst they were racing around and Newton was trying to stop himself from falling off Koi, as he kept spinning around to see what the others were up to, Pythagorus noticed Mr Magnihyde arrive in the stables. It was quite odd, because instead of coming along the tunnel alongside them and through the main door, he suddenly appeared from behind one of the other stable buildings, and darted behind the next one. The only reason Pythagorus had seen him was because he had turned around to help Newton who had fallen off Koi again, and had happened to glance up at the stables as he helped Newton get up.

Pythagorus immediately told Newton what he had seen, as he thought it rather strange behaviour, and the two of them watched their teacher dart down the line of the stable buildings, until he disappeared through the side door into the main stable. He was almost unrecognisable as he was wearing a dark tracksuit and a hat that covered up most of his face. But it was his feet, in a pair of shiny black, pointed cowboy boots with silver tips rather than trainers or riding boots that gave him away.

Whenever they could, the twins glanced at the main stable doors and after about half an hour they spotted him again as he crept out, again via the side door, looking around very cautiously from side to side, before darting behind the nearest building. This time he was carrying a large plastic bag, which was obviously quite heavy from the way he was dragging it along the floor and it created a ripple behind him in the water. He then disappeared back along the same route as before and headed towards the main school buildings.

Pythagorus and Newton were intrigued and they stopped riding for a while with the excuse that their seahorses needed a couple of minutes rest. As they sat resting, they spotted Peter the stable boy, who also came creeping out of the side door of the main stables. He too checked furtively from side to side, before darting back into the stable through the main entrance, head bowed. A couple of minutes later, he strolled back out of the main door smiling with his head held high and carrying a sack of food for the seahorse's tea. He was acting as if everything was normal and nothing unusual had happened.

"Well how extraordinary!" Newton whispered to Pythagorus. "What an earth do you think they were doing?"

"I'm not sure," Pythagorus replied thoughtfully, "but whatever it was, they didn't want anyone to see them."

"Did you see how Mr Magnihyde darted from stable to stable? I think something is going on here," he added "and I think they are up to no good."

"Don't be silly, Pythagorus" responded Newton but sounding a little unsure. "Do you think they realised we were watching them?"

"No," replied Pythagorus "don't worry. I never saw them once look in our direction. They obviously thought we would be too busy riding our seahorses to see anything. I'm sure there must be a simple explanation. Quick, look away," he added quickly, "Peter is coming this way."

The twins then rode off before Peter could get to them and acted as if they had not seen anything unusual. They decided not to say anything to the others, but just to watch both Peter and Mr Magnihyde carefully and see if there were any further developments. They were both very curious and discussed again what they had seen that night when they telephoned their parents. Katie told them that they were imagining things and not to worry but they still went to bed feeling puzzled.

The next day was Sunday, so they quickly finished their homework, had lunch, changed into their normal clothes and dashed off to meet Hugo and Eugene in the main entrance hall for their first visit to town. In the end all of the Octets had been invited but the twins didn't mind. It would make it more fun.
The previous night, Hugo had given them a map of the town to study in the hope that if one of them got lost, they could find their way home. They had all studied it very carefully and only Sofia had forgotten to bring it with her. As requested, they also all carried a couple of the water snails in their pockets, but they didn't know why. They had also brought some of their pocket money in case there were some shops.

As you can imagine, they were very excited and they were all talking at once.

To the twins' delight, when they walked towards the gates at the main school entrance, Ellie was there to greet them as Hugo had asked her to be their water taxi for the afternoon. She nodded her head in greeting to the twins and said hello in her silvery voice. Hugo explained that all she needed for payment was some sugar cubes and as a special treat, a water snail!

"So that is what they are for!" exclaimed Francois.

"Ugh." added Sophia

Eugene laughed and told them Ellie's favourite delicacy was prawns.

Today, Ellie had a large glycon carriage on her back. This was her normal carriage she explained to the twins and that it had been a special treat for them when they had travelled in her conga carriage with Neptune. The twins quickly scrambled up her neck and along her back into the carriage. The others followed much more slowly and some needed to be helped, as this was their first encounter with Ellie. Just as before with the twins she was very gentle with them and they all soon relaxed.

"Fasten your seat belts." instructed Eugene. "Just like at home, seat belts must be worn at all times. Ellie is going to take us for a tour above the city and then over to the city walls on the other side. That way, you should be able to get a good overview of the city layout and it will also enable me to show you where Plympton and Carth are located, which are the other two main towns here in Oceana. We will then stop off in the town centre for a couple of hours so that I can show you where to find the shops. Any questions?" he added.

They all shook their heads, eager to start, and Ellie set off swimming upwards out of the school courtyard, leaving a trail of bubbles behind her. She headed alongside the school for a few minutes before turning past the clock tower towards the city. The clock in the clock tower was stuck at 4.01pm, the precise moment the comet had hit the earth. No one had ever tried to start it working again and so it was left as a reminder of God's power over their world. Ellie then swam above the rocky path they had seen earlier in the week which wound its way down towards the city lights.

On their way, they passed a couple of other electric eel taxis and a shoal of dolphins, all of who greeted them with nods of their heads. They also passed many shoals of brightly coloured fish which were just swimming around.

As Eugene had explained before they set off, Ellie first swam over the shops, houses and the church in the middle of the city, before heading towards the outskirts. When they got to the wall which surrounded the city, they were able to get down for a little while so that they could look at the view. Hugo pointed out some of the places of interest including the lights of Plympton and Carth whilst Eugene gave Ellie a drink and some more sugar lumps. They stood and watched a couple of eel taxis loaded with passengers head off towards one of the other cities and admired the view which stretched out before them.

It was strange looking out over the fields, which must have once been full of grass, or crops or animals. Where the hedges once grew, there was now a row of seaweed stretching up towards the roof and gently waving in the wake of the water as the eels swam by. They could just about hear a splash as the wake the eels had created first hit the wall and then headed out towards the seaweed.

To the left they could see the edge of a coral reef, which had grown once the waters had swept over the land. Here, Eugene explained was where they cultivated some Oyster beds for pearls which were then sold back on the surface. To the right they could see the faint outline of buildings which sat above some mineshafts. Some mines led to oil and gas beds which could be found deep below the surface. Others led to some gold fields, which were closer to the surface. All of these goods were then exported up to the world above, without anyone on the surface realising where they had come from.

A little while later, they returned back to the city. Ellie headed for the centre and they finally came to rest in the middle of the main square, next to the church that they could see from the school. Once they had all disembarked, Ellie swam over to join some other eels, some dolphins and an octopus who were sitting drinking some milkshakes through straws and playing cards at a bar in one corner of the square. From the noise, it looked like the octopus was cheating! The bar was called the "Milky Bar".

Pythagorus and Newton could hear Ellie gossiping with some of the other eels and discussing a mischievous young whale called Monty who was obviously causing them all problems as he kept chasing them every time they left the city. None of the Octets had realised how many sea creatures lived in Oceana with them.

Chapter 13

The Octets then set off to explore the city. Pythagorus, Newton, Bradley and Courtney went with Eugene whilst Francois, Rupert, Archie and Sophia set off with Hugo. They had agreed to meet back in the square in two hours' time in order to have enough time for a quick drink at the Milky Bar before they returned back to school for dinner.

Apart from the Milky bar and the church, there wasn't much else of interest in the main square. There was just a couple of benches, and a large marble statue of Eros, which had once been in the centre of a grand fountain. The twins group headed off down one of the little streets leading away from the square. The streets were very narrow and winding , they were all paved in cobbles so they made quite a noise as the five of them walked along the street.

Eugene took them along a couple of streets and explained that they were heading for the French quarter on the other side of the city. It was called the French quarter as it reminded everybody of Paris in France. The streets were full of tall, thin houses with turrets and wooden shutters on the windows. They must have been about five storeys high. Some of them also had curtains at the windows, and every now and then they were able to see into the front rooms through a chink in the windows. They could see tables and chairs, sofas and fireplaces.

In fact everything looked normal. The only things which made the streets look any different from those in Paris were the vacuum doors in the front of each building which stuck out into the street and had obviously been added later, and of course, the water!

Eventually, they arrived in another smaller square, which was surrounded on all sides by shops of various shapes and sizes. In the centre of the square was another large statue, this time of a blue marble dolphin, which had also once been a fountain. The statue was surrounded by a cluster of tables and chairs, which were packed full with local residents. They were sitting talking and laughing and drinking bottles of coke and cappuccinos – with straws of course. Whenever someone spoke under the water, it created a string of bubbles, so the effect of so many people talking in the water was like a huge firework which has just exploded and was raining down all of its sparkles in the water – but upside down!

In one corner of the square was a cafe called the "Coral Café." It was painted a very pretty pink. There were a number of people standing in front of it talking and drinking coke. The sound of an old Abba record was blaring out of the cafe and it seemed to fill the water in the square with noise. It was obviously the coolest place to be!

The residents themselves looked reasonably normal. They all seemed to be wearing identical water proof tracksuits, but in a multitude of colours, which were easier to walk in through the water than normal clothes. Some were wearing coloured cloaks over their tracksuits and some even had on hats, but quite what purpose these served was a mystery. The gentle waves in the water, which were created as people walked along, kept knocking them off people's heads and they had to keep catching them before they floated away. Some people were of course quite clever and their hats were tied down. Eugene explained that for most of the residents, Sunday was their day off and this was the most popular bar in the city.

"Where do they all work?" asked Courtney.

"Some of them work in the shops and some of them work in the pearl and jewellery factories located near Carth which I showed you earlier." responded Eugene. "Some work down the mines or teach; basically they all do a variety of things. Some of them even commute up to the surface and only come back at weekends but these people are frowned upon" he added, "as they leave their houses empty all week and don't join in as much as the others in the social life of Oceana. Luckily there aren't very many of them."

"The other job they all have to do," he continued, "and this is compulsory, is to take turns at guarding the boundaries of Oceana from intruders. Do you remember seeing them in the sentry boxes at the entrance to the tunnels?" he asked them. "Hopefully you noticed them when you first arrived. They also have to help in the daily patrols of the roof to ensure that no holes are developing in the glycon. In fact, if you look over there," he added pointing up into the water, "you might just be able to make out a patrol."

They all looked up and Pythagorus thought he could just make out some black dots that looked like some small birds in the distance. The others couldn't see anything at all. Eugene then gave them a guided tour around the square and pointed out each of the shops which he thought would be of interest. There was a wonderful looking sweetshop in one of the corners and the sight of the sweets in the window suddenly made them all feel hungry, but they didn't have time to stop. There was a harpoon and fishing shop which had a sign in its window advertising fishing trips in the "warmth" of the Mediterranean. There were a couple of general food shops, two clothes shops, a toyshop, an art shop and at last, the one they had all been waiting for, a magic shop.

Whilst they were walking around the square, looking in the windows of the shops, Newton had also been studying the residents. He had already seen Miss Zephyr in her blue clouds cloak going in and then coming out of the art shop with a couple of bags packed up to the brim with paint and brushes. The bags were all transparent in Oceana so it was easy to see what people has brought and they were all sealed to stop the water from getting into them. She had waved to them as she walked past, dropping all of her bags in the process.

As Eugene and Pythagorus helped her to collect up all of her things, Newton spotted Peter dart into the magic shop. None of the others seemed to see him. Earlier on, Newton had also seen Jock Hunter sitting in the middle of the square drinking coffee with some friends and he had also waved to them as they passed by.

As they continued the tour around the square, Newton also noticed four tall men arrive and sit down in the corner of the Coral café. They looked different from the other residents in the square. Newton assumed they were men as they were covered in long black cloaks and they had pulled the cloaks tightly over their heads so their faces were hidden. They looked a little out of place amongst the other residents in the square and Newton felt a cold shiver run down his back as he looked at them.

Finally, they arrived at "Pinkletons Potions", the magic shop, and with no hesitation Eugene pushed open the door and led them in.

A bell over their heads tinkled their arrival as they walked in through the vacuum doors. Inside the shop it was quite dark and dingy as it was lit by only a few candles. But, once their eyes had got used to the light, they could see that most of the walls were covered in shelves, which in turn were covered in bottles and jars of various shapes and sizes and were in a multitude of colours. They were all labelled, but they didn't understand any of the labels as they were all written in ancient Atlantian language or covered in strange pictures.

"I wonder what's in all of the bottles?" asked Courtney in wonder. "Do you think we have to learn all of these names before our magic can work?"

Someone let out a chuckle as she spoke and so they turned and started walking towards the noise. They could see a counter and behind it another room suddenly appeared out of nowhere. This room had transparent walls and was within the original room and yet it seemed to be larger and was significantly lighter! A couple of steps later they reached the front of the counter, and now they found themselves standing in the middle of the inner room but they could see the outer room behind it. It was a very weird sensation and Courtney jumped back a few steps in surprise. To her initial horror, the inner room, including the others completely disappeared from sight and she found herself back in the gloom of the outer room.

As she stood there, frozen in bewilderment, a hand and an arm came out of nowhere in front of her, grabbed her arm, and Eugene pulled her back into the inner room. Courtney was never more than a few inches away from his side after that. He had become her hero.

"Hello Eugene" said a man who had now appeared behind the counter beaming at them. "I see you've brought your new house recruits to see me at last. I've been expecting you." he added smiling at them.

"Of course Mr Pinkleton." responded Eugene grinning. "Where else would I bring them?"

Mr Pinkleton beamed again. He was not a very tall man and he was quite plump with a round smiling face and red cheeks. He did not have much hair left, except for two grey tufts, which stuck up on either side of his head. It was difficult to guess at his age, but he looked very old.

"Where would you like to begin Eugene?" asked Mr Pinkleton.

"Well I thought it would be a great idea if we gave them their magic starting kit, and perhaps you could go through each item in turn." he suggested.

"Excellent idea." responded Mr Pinkleton. "Excellent." Then clicking his fingers he produced a pair of stepladders from behind him, which were definitely not there before. He climbed up and collected some pre-packed gold boxes from the top shelf of a row of shelves which also seemed to have appeared from nowhere. He opened one of the boxes and tipping the contents out onto the counter started to explain the contents to them one by one. They were all enthralled.

There was an odd assortment of items in the box. Some ordinary items such as marbles, sandpaper, brushes, and superglue, as well as some more exotic items, which of course you always need for magic! There were some bats wings, ground beetle powder, some walrus horn shavings and some shiny fish scales. As he showed them each item he assured them that no animals had been hurt in making these items.

"This is also a step by step beginner's guide to magic." explained Mr Pinkleton holding up a small silver book. "You will need this for your first lessons. It includes your first experiment, which is how to make a laughter potion. Come back and see me when you need the next book." he added with another beaming smile.

He then packed everything back into the box and handed one box to each of them. Somehow, each box he gave them had their own name inscribed in the familiar turquoise writing on the lid of the box. How did he know who they were?

When they peeped inside their boxes, they were amazed at how deep they were and how much more room there seemed to be inside them. In fact, Pythagorus couldn't seem to see the bottom of his box at all which was quite puzzling.

Mr Pinkleton then proceeded to show them some of the other potions and objects he had on his shelves. Whilst the others were engrossed listening to him, and looking and smelling some of the potions, Newton wandered over to one of the other shelves on the opposite wall and started poking around. These bottles were bright blue and some of them had pictures of dolphins painted on them which was what had attracted Newton to them. As he picked up one of the bottles from a lower shelf so as to take a better look at the label, he found himself looking through a small hole into a third room, one that the others didn't seem to be able to see.

This room was the smallest of the three, and this time the shelves were covered in row upon row of books. There were three small tables and chairs in the centre of the room with large "Quiet please, no talking" signs in red writing sitting on each table. It was obviously a small library. Sitting at one of the tables, and talking very quietly were Peter, Mr Magnihyde and two other men in dark cloaks and hoods. Newton wasn't quite sure but he thought they were two of the men he had seen earlier, drinking outside in the corner of the café. Their hoods were now lying on their shoulders, and although they had their backs to him this time Newton could see that it was them again.

At first he couldn't hear a word they were saying as they were all sitting close together at the far end of the room and they were talking very, very quietly. He closed his eyes and concentrated very hard and after a few minutes, he found he was able to make out the odd word or sentence. He overhead phrases such as "Midnight on Sunday", "loaded guns," "stable....," "America" and "glass blower", none of which made any sense to him.

As Newton stood trying to understand their conversation he was suddenly startled by the sound of Pythagorus calling out his name. He jumped up shocked, and then panicked as Peter and Mr Magnihyde turned around also startled and looked straight at him.

Chapter 14

Newton stood frozen to the spot, but somehow they didn't seem to see him as there was no look of recognition on their faces. They shrugged their shoulders and turned back to face each other and continue with their conversation. What Newton didn't know at the time was that there was a picture on their side of the wall immediately in front of him, and his eyes matched those of the picture! As a result they just didn't see him.

"It's only year eight on their first outing," he heard Peter tell the others. "it's nothing to worry about." and they continued with their conversation.

Newton quietly put the potion bottle back on the shelf, somehow in his subconscious memorising the picture and name on the label of the bottle, which was "Crushed anemone petals". He then turned and rejoined the others, in somewhat of a trance and looking very pale.

"Are you alright Newton?" Pythagorus asked, looking at his twin with some concern.

"Ye..es" replied Newton, somewhat hesitantly. "I'll explain later. I'm fine, honest!" he added. He then listened to the others inundating Mr Pinkleton with question after question whilst he slowly recovered from his earlier scare. It quickly became apparent to him that no one else had seen the library or heard anyone else talking, so he decided to ask Mr Pinkleton some questions himself to see if he could find out some more information.

"Where do you keep all of your magic books?" he asked Mr Pinkleton, innocently looking around the shop as he spoke.

"They are kept in the library," he replied, " but I'm afraid you can't go in there, or in fact even see it until you have passed your level two exams."

"Is there anyone in there now?" asked Courtney looking all around her nervously.

Mr Pinkleton glanced in the direction of the shelf where Newton had been standing earlier. "Yes," he said, "there are a couple of people studying in there right now." Eugene didn't bother to listen as he already had access to the room as he had passed his exam in the previous school year.

"Is the entrance in this room?" asked Newton, holding his breath nervously.

"Yes," Mr Pinkleton replied "but there is also a back entrance which leads out directly into the street. But again, you can only see the door once you know the magic spell which makes it appear in the wall. All in good time." he added smiling at them all as he spoke.

"Well I think that's enough for your first visit." interrupted Eugene after about another half hour of questions as he was starting to get bored. "We have a couple of other places we have to visit before we go back to school."

"I'm sure I'll see you all again soon." responded Mr Pinkleton smiling at them all. "I hope you enjoy your first magic lesson tomorrow," he added with a chuckle.

They took a couple of steps towards the outer door, clutching a bag containing their boxes tightly as the inner room and Mr Pinkleton disappeared from sight, and they found themselves back in the darkness of the outer room. They then set off again around the square as Eugene led them towards the art shop where Miss Zephyr had been shopping earlier. On the way, they saw Hugo and the other

Octets heading towards Mr Pinkleton's shop. They all waved to each other as they crossed the square.

Try as he might, Newton couldn't see the magic entrance to the library anywhere.

Miss Montage ran the art shop, which was called "The Trompe L'oeil". Her shop was filled not only with all the art materials you would ever require including an immense range of paints, but also a collection of semi-precious stones. Miss Montage also had a box of art materials to give them, again with their name inscribed on them. Francois had beamed with pleasure when he had received his box earlier in the afternoon. This time when they opened it, they could see the bottom of the box as it was not bottomless like the magic boxes they had been given earlier by Mr Pinkleton.

"These are a gift from me to you for you to use in your art lessons." explained Miss Montage smiling at them. "I'd also like you to pick up a stone for you to keep in your study rooms. These will hopefully bring you peace and tranquility and will help you to channel your energy."

She pointed to a glass box on the counter, which was full of polished stones in a mixture of shapes and colours. She got some of them out of the glass box to show them and as she moved them around they sparkled and lit up the room with rays of light.

Pythagorus and Newton were both immediately attracted to two blue water sapphires. They decided they would be put in a prime position on the table in their study room. Courtney picked up a piece of yellow topaz and Bradley picked a piece of black Jet. Archie, who had been in earlier had picked a piece of amber to match his hair. Sophia had picked a small diamond, and was disappointed to hear that they were worthless in Oceana. Rupert had picked a piece of heliotrope, also known as a blood stone, whilst Francois, who had fallen in love with everything in the shop, had picked a piece of rose quartz.

Miss Montage explained that there was no point taking them home in the holidays as the earth's atmosphere would instantly destroy or dampen their colour and they would lose their sparkle. She added that she would be happy to look after them in the holidays if they wanted.

Once they had chosen their stones, Eugene took them to the café in the courtyard to have a lemonade whist they waited for the others. They soon arrived, also carrying their parcels. Whilst they were waiting, Courtney had taken the opportunity to nip into the sweet shop to buy some boiled sweets and lemon sherbets, which she happily handed around. They then sat there discussing what they had seen and done, chewing the delicious sweets and drinking their lemonades.

All except Newton who sat there lost in thought, but Pythagorus covered for him whenever anyone asked him a question. As they sat there Newton saw Peter and Mr Magnihyde appear out of nowhere close to the magic shop, creep around the square in the shadows of the buildings and head towards the eel taxis.

A few minutes later he also saw the two dark strangers cross the square, shortly joined by the other two, who had obviously been waiting somewhere for them. They then headed off in a different direction, this time towards Carth.

"Well it's nearly time to go back to school." said Hugo. "Do you think you can find your way back to Ellie at the Milky Bar by yourselves?" he asked them.

"Of course we can." they responded in unison.

"Good," he said, "Eugene and I have to pop to the Saddlers in Princes square to pick up some new riding boots we ordered last term, so we will meet you back in the Milky Bar in about half an hour. Now are you sure?"

"No problem." said Rupert confidently, sounding a bit huffed that they were questioning their ability to find the main square.

They finished their drinks and then headed back to find the Milky Bar, maps in hand. Rupert thought it was easy and immediately led the way pointing to a church spire in the distance, and, despite Courtney's protests that they were going the wrong way, strode off towards it. The others followed him but just as Courtney had predicted, it was the wrong way and they found themselves standing in a much smaller and darker courtyard.

So, they turned around and went back the way that they had come but again took the wrong turn and within a few more minutes they were completely lost. They spent the next hour wandering around the city looking for the centre and the main square in vain, Sophia complaining all the time because her feet hurt and her boxes were heavy!

When they finally found the Milky Bar, they were all tired and getting cold and they didn't appreciate being shouted at by Eugene. When they hadn't turned up at the Milky Bar as expected, he had become very worried about them and had sent Hugo and a couple of the dolphins to look for them. Now that they had returned, he sent another dolphin to find Hugo who arrived a little while later looking very cross indeed. Needless to say he gave them another telling off!

Grateful to see Ellie at last, the Octets clambered up into her carriage and let her take them back home. By the time they got back to school, they were over an hour and a half late and were greeted by a very anxious Neptune who scolded them all rather badly for being late. He had already received a message from a dolphin that Ellie had sent on in front of them that they had all been found safe and well, so luckily for them he had made sure that some dinner had been kept warm for them.

They were all very tired by the day's events so after dinner they headed back to their own study rooms early. It was surprising how tiring it was to walk in the water when you weren't used to it! Pythagorus and Newton however didn't go to sleep immediately as Newton was desperate to tell Pythagorus everything he had seen and heard in Mr Pinkletons library.

Pythagorus was amazed and they spent some time trying to guess what Peter and Mr Magnihyde were plotting, and what was in the bag Mr Magnihyde had taken from the stables. They couldn't however come up with any good ideas or plausible explanations and decided that further investigation was required. How they would achieve that was something they would decide later. Sleep and possibly strange dreams beckoned first!

Chapter 15

The twins woke up bright and early the next morning, eager for the school day to start. They had decided already that they were going to test Mr Magnihyde to see how much he knew of the library and whether he would admit to knowing Peter. Peter was also going to be subtly questioned about his magic knowledge. At the same time they were going to watch them both to see if they did meet up again or do anything else suspicious. Unfortunately, it would be a couple of days before they had lessons with either of them, but, they were both determined to find out more.

The next few days seemed to pass by very quickly. That first morning, they had received a letter from their mum full of news about home. For a little while it made them feel quite homesick, especially when she mentioned having seen Harry and Billy playing football at the weekend. They loved their new school but they had told Katie that they missed their two friends, and were looking forward to seeing them again at Christmas. Luckily, school was so much fun, the twins didn't feel sad for too long.

Lessons continued as normal, well as normal as they could be considering where they were! Mr Drill, they had soon decided, was the horriblest teacher of all as he had sprung a 50 question history test on them when they arrived for their second lesson with him. He just wanted to know how much they all knew, he informed them with not even a flicker of a smile.

"Tests are good for the soul." he had then said, smirking at them. They were not amused! Nor was he however when he had finished marking their papers!

They had also started their magic lessons with Artimas. The first few lessons were a bit boring as they had to have a crash course on Atlantica, its history and its people. They also had to learn both the language and symbols of magic, in order to be able to read the labels on the magic potions and understand some of the magic spells.

The language was completely different to English and it took them all a while before they could start to recognise the words let alone speak them! It wasn't long however before they started learning how to put the ingredients together and the lessons became much more interesting.

Things were quite sophisticated these days as they firstly put the ingredients into a plastic container and then cooked them in a microwave! The traditional method of a cauldron and a lit fire were long gone! Archie and Newton, who had been paired off in their first lesson had been a little too enthusiastic with their laughter potion and hadn't stopped laughing for about a week! Artimas was not so amused by their antics.

The music and drama clubs continued at quite a pace. Miss Clang was determined that the choir should perform the best Christmas concert ever this year, and they had not a moment to lose. As a result she expected them to attend hour-long rehearsals every other day. Although she was fun and they all loved singing, they were all hoarse by the end of each week. Verity told them she was always like this with year 8.

The rehearsals for Romeo and Juliet with Miss Zephyr were not quite as intense, but were equally long. Francois loved spending time rehearsing and he and Sophia spent many an hour huddled in a corner or in the living room running through their lines. Sophia was convinced that Francois fancied her and would ask her out at any minute. Francois was of course totally oblivious to this, not being at all interested in girls yet! Archie meanwhile seemed to change day by day as his part in the play, although small, gave him more and more confidence.

Bradley, Newton and Pythagorus had soon found themselves roped into helping with the play and they could often be seen backstage or filling in as actors in the crowd scenes.

Whenever the twins and Bradley had an opportunity however they could be found engrossed with one of the sporting activities, which were their first loves. They were often found at lunchtimes riding their seahorses and practising their maneuvers. Bradley and Pythagorus were always racing against each other across the courtyard and they became more and more competitive as the weeks went by. Newton in the meantime spent most of his time practising his dive-bombing and tackling skills, sometimes using Koi as an opponent or treating Bradley and Pythagorus as moving targets as they raced along. It was quite scary to watch him suddenly attacking them with a nose dive!

In their next chemistry lesson, Pythagorus had casually asked Mr Magnihyde if he had visited town yet, and was rather flummoxed when he told him that he had not yet left the school premises. Pythagorus knew that he was lying, but he had apparently been too busy with his experiments in the school laboratory!

Another time; when Newton found himself alone with Peter in the stables whilst he was waiting for the other two to return from stabling their horses, he had asked Peter whether he had ever studied magic or passed any magic exams. Peter had told him no, unfortunately he had never learnt to read Atlantian or studied magic, but he was hoping to learn some soon. Newton offered to help teach him what he had learnt so far which wasn't much, but Peter hurriedly explained that it was already arranged and had rushed away before Newton could ask him any more questions.

The twins had quickly hit a dead end in both cases and they were very disappointed.

However they were still determined to discover the truth and so from then on, and at every available opportunity the twins watched both Peter and Mr Magnihyde like hawks, but to their disappointment nothing else strange happened. That is until about three weeks later.

One Sunday afternoon, Newton, Pythagorus, Archie and Courtney were practising water hockey in the water tank. Francois and Sophia were as usual tucked away in the corner of the living room rehearsing their parts for the play. Rupert was sitting with them, quietly reading a book, whilst Bradley was practising with Pegasus down in the stables. Newton was feeling very exuberant and was dashing around the tank, dive bombing the others and then veering away just at the very last moment.

"I wish you'd stop doing that Newton," shouted Courtney quite crossly. "I keep thinking you are going to hit me."

She was getting fed up of having to suddenly jump out of his way and she was developing rather a large headache. She wasn't used to Newton doing this as she normally played in goal at the end of the tank and so never got attacked in this way.

Newton was taken aback; not only at being shouted at and her words, but also by the fact that she had questioned his diving skills!

So much so that he momentarily lost concentration. This was not a good idea as he was in the middle of a particularly steep and fast descent aiming straight at Archie, who was walking along the bottom of the tank chatting with Pythagorus and looking in the opposite direction. They were busy discussing the latest football results sent to them by Archie's dad and in particular

Manchester United's brilliant performance on Saturday, whilst they went to collect the puck which had just gone offside.

The next second and despite all his best efforts to stop, Newton and his hockey stick collided with Archie knocking him flat to the ground, with Newton's hockey stick ending up wrapped around his head. It had immediately broken in two on impact. Although Pythagorus was closer, Newton had just missed landing on top of him whilst his hockey stick had skimmed the top of his head by just a couple of inches. Newton immediately jumped up, but Archie didn't and he lay there on the bottom of the tank motionless in front of them.

"Oh my God!" said Courtney clasping her hands to her mouth in horror. "Newton, what an earth have you done? Have you killed him?"

"Of course I haven't." snapped Newton desperately hoping that Archie would jump up at these words, but he didn't. Newton began to prod him with the broken hockey stick but Archie still didn't move.

"Quick," said Pythagorus who was starting to panic. "I think he is unconscious, so we must get him out of the water in case he can't breathe properly. Come on" he added, "help me lift him up."

Luckily for them, Archie was not very heavy and the three boys were able to lift him up with ease. They quickly got him out of the water and up onto the balcony where Pythagorus started to apply the first aid techniques they had learnt at their previous school for when people have stopped breathing.

First he put Archie in the recovery position, which is on your side with your chin forward to keep the airways open, and he then tried to pump the water out of his mouth.

Pythagorus was relieved that he did not have to give Archie the kiss of life as within a few seconds, Archie coughed, spat out a mouthful of water and started breathing again. He looked very pale and lay on the floor, groaning. Newton in the meantime stood rooted to the spot, unable to move as he watched his brother save Archie's life.

"Newton quick, go and get some warm towels and a dressing gown for Archie and our clothes." commanded Pythagorus, who was by now shivering with cold. "I think we ought to take Archie to see Matron."

When his brother didn't move, still frozen in shock, he shouted at him "NOW Newton, NOW."

At this, Newton finally snapped out of his trance and dashed off to the changing rooms to collect them. They hastily put on their clothes, wrapped Archie up in some of the warm towels and dressing gown, picked him up again and headed off towards matron's room.

None of them had been in there yet, but Pythagorus had remembered that her room was next to Artimas' room in the main entrance hall. It was quite a distance for them to carry Archie, who seemed to get heavier with every step especially when they climbed the stairs, but they soon arrived at her room.

When Courtney knocked on the door, they were very relieved when Matron eventually opened the door. No one in the school knew her real name so she was only ever called matron. As it was Sunday, they had been worried that it might be her day off and she could have been shopping in town. Matron was plump and jolly looking, with a kind face and a warm smile and she was wearing a crisp, white starched uniform. They immediately knew that she would make Archie better.

Matron helped them lift Archie on to her "operating table" as it was called and started to check and fuss over him, whilst Pythagorus and Courtney told her what had happened. Archie was starting to come around by this time. He was completely disorientated but kept trying to talk so between them all they were making quite a commotion.

Newton stood back a little from the others and waited just inside the doorway with the door remaining ajar as there wasn't really enough room for them all to fit into Matron's office. As he stood there, still in shock, he heard a strange gurgling noise coming from Artimas' room followed by a soft thud. Newton turned to look at Artimas' room but the door was firmly closed and he couldn't see anything amiss. So, he turned back to look at Archie, who by now was protesting to Matron that there was nothing wrong with him at all, and could she please turn off those flashing lights above his head. (There weren't any!)

Archie couldn't say the words in the right order and was obviously still suffering from concussion. Whilst Courtney and Pythagorus continued to explain to Matron what had happened, a large bump was forming in front of them on the back of his head. Poor Newton remained standing in the doorway riddled with guilt.

Then as he stood there, he heard Artimas' door open very, very quietly and very, very slowly behind him and some sixth sense told him not to immediately turn around. Remembering how he could hear the conversations in the library and also Koi talking to him when he concentrated hard, he began to concentrate on trying to see who was behind him without actually turning around to look.

When that didn't initially work he closed his eyes tight to enable him to concentrate even more and to block out the sound of the others talking.

Chapter 16

Slowly a vision of someone's aura came into Newton's mind although he couldn't see who it belonged to. The aura was dense and black and seemed to shimmer with evil and Newton shivered when he felt it start to appear in his mind.

Then, suddenly, he sensed the person's thoughts come tumbling out over the space between them.

"Gently now." they seemed to be saying. "That silly boy doesn't know it's you behind the door. Just creep away up the stairs and he'll never know you were here."

Newton realised with a jolt that they were Peter's thoughts as somehow the thoughts seemed to speak in the same voice and tone as their master. There was no mistake. Newton didn't move a muscle and continued to pretend to watch the scene in front of him as he sensed rather than saw Peter slowly creep up the stairs.

It was only when he felt him reach the top stair letting out a sigh of relief and when he was just about to head away along the corridor that Newton turned his head slightly in order to glance up the stairs.

He was right, it was Peter, and he watched him disappear from sight. Newton was stunned by everything he had seen and heard and felt suddenly overcome with exhaustion.

"Pythagorus," whispered Newton to his brother rather loudly "we have to go somewhere NOW."

Both Pythagorus and Courtney immediately stopped talking to Matron and looked at him in surprise, sensing the urgency in his manner and hearing the command in his voice.

"Yes, yes." interrupted Matron not looking at them, and seemingly oblivious to Newton's odd statement. "Do run along now as you are disturbing my patient. Come back and see us in a few hours time and I'm sure you'll find him much improved."

With that she ushered them out of her room impatiently and went back to tend to Archie.

"Courtney," said Newton urgently, "please don't ask me any questions right now just trust me."

"Run down to the stables as fast as you can and tell Bradley to wait for Peter the stable boy and then follow him wherever he goes." he whispered. "Tell him it's a matter of life and death and not to let him out of his sight. But it's very, very important that he doesn't let Peter know that he is being followed."

"Tell him," he added "to take Jock's shell phone with him if he can, and we will catch him up or pass him a message as soon as we can. If you see Neptune on your way can you tell him that I need to talk to him URGENTLY and then send him here. Now go on, quickly." he commanded.

Courtney nodded her head started to ran off. She had been tempted to ask Newton lots of questions, and indeed at one point to tell him to do it himself when he started to order her around, but something in his voice and the look on his face stopped her. Whatever it was, it was obviously serious so she ran as fast as she could.

"Oh and Courtney" Newton called after her urgently, "go and see if you can find Neptune and Eugene and bring them here as well."

With that Bradley rushed up the staircase to see if he could find them.

"Pythagorus" said Newton finally turning to his brother and holding up his hand to stop him from talking. "Don't ask me any questions just concentrate very hard and help me call Neptune in your thoughts."

"We have to find him fast" he added.

The twins then stood for a couple of minutes and yelled for Neptune in their heads. Newton didn't know if his uncle could hear them but it was worth a try!

"Now follow me." he said.

Newton then led his brother to Artimas' room. He gently knocked on the door, but when they heard no answer, he cautiously pushed open the door and they slowly crept in. The sight that met their eyes when they entered Artimas' room was almost unbelievable. The room was a complete and utter mess with books and papers strewn everywhere. It looked like either a whirlwind had attacked the room, or there had been a tremendous fight, or perhaps even both!

They gasped in horror at the sight of the mess and looked at each other with big wide eyes.

"We'd better go and find Artimas," said Newton to Pythagorus turning to leave the room.

"No, wait a moment Newton," replied Pythagorus grabbing his brother on his arm, "I thought I heard a noise." With that he walked towards Artimas' desk and let out another deep gasp.

"Oh no." he said looking very shocked as he bent down behind the desk. "Quick Newton, come here. Look its

Artimas and I think he's been hurt. He's not moving and I can see drops of blood on the floor." he added.

Newton then rushed forward to find Artimas lying on his front with his face on the floor. He had a silk scarf tied around his head, which was acting as a form of gag and another scarf was tied tightly around his wrists. His large ebony chair was strapped to his back, and was so heavy, that now he had fallen, he could not move and he was pinned to the ground.

When he heard them speak he let out a muffled moan.

The two boys knelt beside him and began to untie the chair but some of the knots were so tight they struggled to undo them. Pythagorus then remembered seeing a gold letter opener on Artimas' desk when they had been in his room earlier in the term. Luckily, it was still there and so they were quickly able to cut the remaining knots and lift off the chair. They then cut the scarves tied around Artimas' head and wrists and helped him to sit up in his chair. He was moaning and muttering all the time but they couldn't understand a word he said.

Newton fetched him some water from the sink in his room so that Artimas could have a drink. He didn't like the look of the gash on Artimas' forehead, which was now bleeding quite heavily, or the fact that he was gasping for air and clutching his chest. He was obviously quite badly hurt.

"Peter…" mumbled Artimas, "Oceana, Ruby of Life." He started to look around him anxiously, obviously looking for something.

The twins looked at each other in bewilderment. What an earth was he talking about?

"Staff," mumbled Artimas, stretching out his hand and clucking his fingers as if requesting them to give it to him, "get my staff." he told them anxiously.

The twins searched the room and eventually found the staff buried under some papers in the corner of the room. Pythagorus picked it up and handed it back to Artimas. They also found a large, heavy stick with blood on its side, which had obviously been used to knock him out. They decided that this must have been what Mr Magnihyde was carrying in his sack when they had seen him a few days before in the stables.

"We'd better go and get Matron." Pythagorus said to Neptune.

"Wait." commanded Artimas who was starting to recover his voice now that he had taken a sip of water and was staring blindly at his staff. "My Ruby.. Where is the Ruby Of Life?" He turned the staff towards the twins and showed them the empty hole on the top of the staff where the ruby had once lain.

He tried to get up but fell back heavily into the chair clutching at his head and groaning.

"Boys, you must find it." he said anxiously. "Peter has stolen it. Hurry boys, hurry. There is not much time. Remember if the ruby is taken out of Oceana, our world will be destroyed. Now hurry!!" he finished, waving at them to go.

Chapter 17

Newton and Pythagorus looked at each other, shocked for a few seconds. "Mr Magnihyde and Peter." they said in unison. "They must be behind this!" they added.

At this news Artimas sank back in the chair, both confused by the news and exhausted.

However before he could ask any questions, Newton and Pythagorus rushed out of the room to find Neptune. In the process they bumped straight into Eugene, who was coming down the staircase and was heading for the sixth form corridor, knocking all the books out of his hand.

"Artimas is injured and the ruby has gone!" the twins told him in unison, the words coming out so quickly that Eugene could only just understand them. "We think its Peter and Mr Magnihyde who have taken it but we've got to go and find Neptune. Please get matron to look after Artimas, but if you see Neptune, please tell him to meet us in the main entrance in 10 minutes. It's really, really urgent."

With that, they both rushed up the stairs, two at a time.

Eugene picked up his books and watched them go shaking his head in amusement as he thought they were playing a prank on him. It was only when he heard the sound of a moan coming from Artimas' open room, and went in to find him now semi-conscious in his chair, still heavily bleeding from the gash and very pale, that Eugene realised with a jolt that the twins were telling the truth.

Eugene dashed over to matron and almost had to drag her over to Artimas' room as she was still fussing over Archie and didn't initially believe him. She let out a scream of shock when she saw Artimas but quickly set to work checking his injuries before calling for the local doctor. Eugene then helped her carry Artimas into her room, which was by now becoming rather overcrowded.

Luckily, he was soon able to leave them and he dashed off to find Neptune who he knew was in the houseroom to tell him what had happened to Artimas and to see if he could explain the twin's very odd statements about the ruby. On his way he collected Verity, who was reading a book in her study.

Newton and Pythagorus meanwhile had dashed off to their room to change. They were still damp from their swim, so they dried themselves quickly and changed into their tracksuits. Newton collected some things into a rucksack which he thought they might need, including their daggers, some torches, their shell phones and all of their water snails.

Pythagorus in the meantime explained what had happened to Artimas and Archie to Rupert, Francois and Sophia who were all in the living room and he made them quickly change into their tracksuits so that they could come with them. They were shocked and inundated him with questions but he didn't have time to tell them anymore.

Pythagorus then opened the floor in their living room and called for Goldie and Koi, who thankfully arrived very quickly.

"Meet us at the front entrance in 10 minutes," he told them "and try and get Ellie and the other seahorses. Has Peter arrived in the stable yet?" he asked them speaking very quickly, "And is Bradley following him? Have you seen Mr Magnihyde anywhere?"

The two seahorses seemed to nod or shake their heads to each question, and Pythagorus was convinced that they were telling him that Peter had set off on his own seahorse and Bradley was following him. There was however no sign of Mr Magnihyde. They also wanted to know what was happening, but Pythagorus told them Newton would explain shortly, so the seahorses dashed off to look for Ellie so that they could all meet them at the main entrance.

Luckily for them, Eugene and Verity had managed to find Neptune very quickly, and by the time the twins and the others arrived at the main entrance, they were all waiting for them and desperate to find out what was happening. As the twins started to explain everything they'd seen and heard over the past few weeks, Courtney arrived breathing very deeply, having just run there and back from the stables to find Bradley. So they had to start all over again.

When they had finished explaining everything that they had seen and heard over the past few weeks, Courtney confirmed that she had left Bradley hiding in the stables and waiting for Peter. She was a bit huffed when Pythagorus told her that they already knew that Peter had now left and they thought that Bradley was following him. What a waste of effort running all the way back she thought. A few minutes later, as she stood there still sulking, Ellie, Goldie and Koi arrived, together with Eugene and Verity's two horses, Florin and Guinevere and Neptune's pet dolphin Plato.

"Where do you think Peter and Mr Magnihyde have gone?" asked Sophia "and what do you think they are going to do with the ruby?"

"My guess" answered Neptune "is that they are trying to get the ruby to the upper world. They think that they would make an absolute fortune if they sold it on the black market but of course it can never leave Oceana without being destroyed." Some of the others nodded their heads in agreement.

116

"Don't they realise that they will destroy Oceana?" gasped Rupert. Even he, who had little time for the school, looked shocked at this thought.

"I don't expect they care very much." replied Eugene thoughtfully. "Neptune, do you think they will use the tunnels to try to escape because we could contact the sentries. They could then lock the gates to prevent them from escaping that way." he added.

"I don't think it will be that simple." sighed Neptune. "My guess is that they will try and use one of the back exits, but we will phone the sentries on the way and warn them."

"Where are the back exits?" asked Francois. By now they were all utterly intrigued as no one had mentioned these before.

"Well," Neptune replied, "there are a couple of exits through the pipes in the oil mines and along the railway lines, which are used to carry the gold to the surface. There is also an old legend that says that there is a door buried somewhere deep within the Oyster pearl beds near Carth." he added thoughtfully, scratching his chin as he spoke.

"But" he continued, "no one has ever found it, and we don't know where it leads to in the upper world. In fact, it is said that a previous king of Oceana, who was not a good man, cast a magic spell over it to hide it a few centuries ago."

"One day" he continued "he fell in love with a young girl from the upper world, kidnapped her and then made her his slave. Somehow she managed to escape from him and fled back into her own world using this door, and he never found her again. The legend says that he was so angry and jealous, that he spun a magic wall to cover up the door and he banned anyone from ever mentioning it or the young girl ever again."

"To my knowledge," he finished thoughtfully "it has never been seen or used since."

"Wow," said Sophia completely enthralled by the story, "it sounds fascinating. Was she beautiful, Oh do tell us more?"

"Not now you stupid girl!" interrupted Rupert giving her a scornful look. "We can't stand here listening to old stories and gossiping. We've got to go after them."

"Who are you calling stupid?" responded Sophia angrily, her body tensing up for a fight.

"I think," interjected Newton moving to stand between them, so as to stop the row that was brewing rapidly, "we should try and find that exit. Don't forget," he suddenly added, "that I overheard them discussing a glass blower. Maybe there is a connection between that and the pearl factories they also mentioned?"

"But Neptune just said that no-one knows where the exit is Newton." said Pythagorus giving his brother a quizzical look, "what makes you think they have found it?"

"I don't know why, but some sixth sense tells me they have." Newton told his brother, "You've just got to trust me on this one," he added.

□

Chapter 18

Pythagorus studied his brother carefully, and considered this for a few minutes and then replied somewhat pensively, "Ok Newton, if you are sure about this." Newton nodded his head. They then both looked at Neptune, not quite sure of the next step.

"In that case," said Neptune "I think it would be best if we separate into two groups, then hopefully we will stand a better chance of finding both of them, and of course, the ruby. Verity," he commanded now having taken charge of the situation. "You go with Ellie and take Pythagorus, Courtney, Sophia, Francois and Rupert with you. You must find Bradley who is hopefully following Peter by now, and help him catch Peter and, if he is with him, Mr Magnihyde, before they leave Oceana."

"I am sure" he added encouragingly "that there will be enough of you to catch them, but I will send messages to the sentry boxes to close the tunnels immediately, and the patrols to keep an eye out for them. You should have plenty of back up from them, but keep in touch with the shell phones if there is a problem, and of course let us know if you catch them." he added.

"Eugene, Newton and I will head off towards the oyster beds and the pearl factory." Neptune sighed, shaking his head, and then added, "In many ways I think we are going on a wild goose chase, but something in the back of my mind says that Newton might be right, but I don't know why."

He then picked up his phone and started to contact the sentries.

"Can't I come with you Neptune please!" begged Courtney to their surprise a few minutes later and just as they were setting off. "I'm sure I can help you find the old door." she added looking coyly at Eugene. He shuffled his feet and looked totally embarrassed at the look she had given him. Neptune who was totally oblivious to this as he was still talking quietly to the guards in the sentry boxes, agreed to her request just to keep the peace, and so as to not waste any more time.

So, Pythagorus and Verity jumped onto their seahorses, whilst Sophia, Rupert and Francois climbed up on to Ellie's back. They had to hold on to her humps very tightly as she hadn't had time to strap on a carriage, but she promised them that she would swim very carefully. They then rushed off towards the stables to find Bradley, but when they got there, they found that he had indeed already left and so they presumed that he was following Peter.

Jock Hunter was in the stables when they arrived, and Pythagorus quickly explained to him what had happened. Jock looked puzzled when they finished explaining but told them that he had seen Bradley head upwards towards Plympton but he hadn't seen Peter for some hours. When they checked Peter's room above the stables, to their dismay all of his things were gone and they then discovered that his seahorse was also missing from his stable.

Jock was shocked, but was by now convinced by their story, (he was originally rather sceptical), and agreed that he would first go and check that both Artimas and Archie were alright. He would then collect up some of the other sixth formers to form a backup team and they would follow them shortly towards Plympton.

Jock also gave them a long piece of rope, which he thought they might find useful and they could perhaps use to catch Peter. Ellie meanwhile agreed that she would leave a silvery trail in the water for them to follow.

With that arranged the six of them set off in hot pursuit of Bradley and Peter and they all agreed that they would keep in touch by their shell phones.

Meanwhile, Newton, Eugene, Neptune and Courtney set off towards Carth and the mines and oyster beds. Courtney did not have her own seahorse with her, so she sat on the back of Plato with Neptune. Plato was rather slippery so she hugged onto Neptune very tightly, so tight in fact that he could only just breathe! As they swam along, other dolphins and some wild seahorses drew up beside them. Neptune seemed to issue them all with instructions as they all rushed off again in different directions.

"Any news yet?" asked Newton after he recognised one of the dolphins which had returned and then dashed off again in the same direction.

"No, there is no sign of Mr Magnihyde yet," responded Neptune, "but apparently Bradley has set off after Peter, and the others are about half an hour behind him. It's a lot of time to make up, but their seahorses are fast so hopefully they should just about catch Peter up before he reaches the tunnels."

The oyster beds and pearl factories, which lay deep within the coral reef were a long way away, about a distance of 20 nautical miles, and Neptune told them that he thought it would take them about two hours to get there, provided they didn't have to stop anywhere on the way.

"Newton, will you be alright riding that sort of distance?" asked Eugene kindly after about twenty minutes knowing that Newton must have ridden his seahorse no more than half a dozen times, and never for longer than half an hour in one stretch. By now they were a long way from school and heading deep into the ocean.

"I'll be fine," responded Newton through gritted teeth. He was struggling to stay on Koi not only because he was going very fast, but because of the power of the waves in the open water. The waves had initially looked so pretty when they had first approached them, but now seemed to be constantly trying to knock him off!

They rode on silently for about another half an hour, slowly leaving the lights of the school and the town behind them, until there was nothing around them but a thick, deep blackness.

"Can't we use our torches?" whispered Courtney, who was rather afraid of the dark. "How do we know we are heading in the right direction?" She jumped and nearly fell off Pluto as another dolphin appeared out of nowhere, brushing her leg as it swam past.

"Don't worry about that" replied Neptune kindly. "The dolphins and seahorses don't need light to see where they are going as they use a form of radar, and they all know the way both to the oyster beds and the mines. Also, we don't want to use the torches in case we attract attention or alert Mr Magnihyde that we are following him. It's also best that we save them just in case we need them later on in the mines."

Courtney started shivering at this point, suddenly wishing that that she had taken the easier route and followed Peter with the others.

"Have you decided whether we are going to the gold mines first or the pearl factories?" asked Eugene.

"Well I know that Newton is convinced that he has gone to the pearl factories, but it is a long shot and I think we ought to check out the gold mines first." responded Neptune. "If he hasn't gone that way, we will have only wasted about an hour, but at least we would know for sure. Do you agree Newton?" Neptune added.

"Yes, and no" Newton replied thoughtfully. "I know that what you are saying is sensible, but I am still convinced that he is heading towards the hidden door in the pearl factories. But if you think that we will not waste much time checking the mines first then I guess it would be a sensible thing to do." he added not sounding very convinced at all.

Just then the silence around them was shattered by the ringing sound of his mobile phone. As a joke one day, and to Newton's complete embarrassment, Pythagorus had fiddled about with the ring tone on his phone, so that it now played "Baa Baa Black Sheep" instead of a normal ring tone. Newton hadn't been able to figure out how to change it back so the unusual sounds of the nursery rhyme filled the water around them.

Newton grabbed the phone out of his pocket, and angrily yelled "hello" down the phone to his brother (he knew it just had to be him!).

"Shush" whispered his brother, "we have finally caught up with Bradley and we can just about see Peter in the distance. He is only about a half mile ahead of us." The water was not as black when you were near the glycon roof, and so it was much easier to see through the water. "There is no sign of Mr Magnihyde anywhere" he added, "but we are holding back just in case he arrives. What does Neptune want us to do?"

Newton then passed the phone to Neptune who responded. "Stay back as far as you dare until Peter reaches the tunnels, just in case Mr. Magnihyde joins him. Then grab him and take him back to school. But" he instructed "You must search him first to see if he's got the ruby and hopefully he'll tell you where Mr Magnihyde has gone. Then take him straight to Artimas - he'll know what to do with him if he won't talk to you."

"Whatever you do" he added "don't ring us again until you've caught him or both of them or even the ruby itself."

"If we don't hear from you, we'll contact you in about an hour. Good luck." Neptune added ringing off.

"Newton" Neptune than said sternly, handing him back the phone. "Sort out that ring tone immediately. I just hope to God that Mr Magnihyde didn't hear us." he added.

"I'm sorry, but I can't Uncle Neptune," responded Newton sounding very cross and despondent all at the same time. "I don't know how to."

"Don't worry Newton," said Courtney suddenly feeling rather sorry for him. "I'll fix it for you" She then fiddled about with the keys for a few minutes and then told them that she had switched off the sound. The phone would now vibrate instead of ringing, so he would be able to feel rather than hear if it rang again. Gratefully, Newton put it away in his pocket.

And so for the next hour, both "teams" quietly chased their prey!

In the meantime back at the school, Jock Hunter had managed to persuade Matron to allow him to visit Artimas alone for a few minutes whilst they waited for the doctor to arrive. He explained to a shocked, but still dazed Artimas everything Pythagorus had told him and they agreed that Jock should set off as fast as he could to help Bradley and the others catch Peter and hopefully Mr. Magnihyde.

At that point they didn't know anything about the quest for the hidden door, or the trip to the mines, because in all of the excitement, Pythagorus had forgotten to tell him!

124

Somewhat reluctantly, Artimas agreed to stay at the school and await developments. He would have the unenviable task of warning the residents of Oceana if the Ruby was not found, and making sure the evacuation program they had practised many times before was put into motion, before the roof collapsed. He had a splitting headache, the gash across his eye was throbbing, and he was suddenly starting to feel very, very old. But if the time came, none of this would stop him from leading the evacuation.

Jock reluctantly left him, and went to gather up some sixth formers. He had known Artimas since he was a child and he had never seen him look so shocked and down hearted before. The rest of the sixth formers already knew that Artimas was hurt, and somehow seemed to know that they were on the brink of something terrible. Bad news always travelled fast!

So they had gathered together with Miss Zephyr in her room and were anxiously looking out of her windows for some sort of sign or activity. Miss Zephyr was trying to reassure them that nothing was wrong, but to no avail. They were very relieved when Jock arrived looking for them and before long they were saddling their own seahorses, ready to help the others catch the two criminals.

Miss Zephyr and about a dozen of the sixth formers reluctantly agreed to stay behind to guard Artimas and help him as best as they could. It was agreed that the younger students were not to be told anything at this stage to avoid any panic. They would however warn all of the staff.

Chapter 19

Pythagorus and the others within his group were surprised at how quickly they had caught up with Bradley. It would seem that Peter, perhaps not wanting to attract any attention and oblivious to the fact that Newton had seen him earlier leaving Artimas's room, or the fact that he was being followed was riding very slowly, as if out for a Sunday drive. He was heading over Plympton and towards the tunnels beyond. It would seem that there were tunnels all over Oceana.

As agreed with Neptune on the phone, they kept their distance, hoping that Peter wouldn't spot them. All the time they scanned the water around them, searching for a sign of Mr Magnihyde, but he was nowhere to be seen.

"How do you think we should go about capturing him?" Sophia asked about a half hour later. It was the question they were all asking themselves. "Pythagorus, Verity do you have a plan?"

"Well" replied Pythagorus "I've been thinking. If I remember properly, and Ellie please tell me if I'm wrong, there are two tunnels this side of the entrance to the upper world, and one tunnel on the other side which is actually in the upper world. So, we need to catch Peter before he reaches the third tunnel."

"I think once he reaches the first tunnel, we should catch him up, surround him, and then drag him back to school. It should be easier there because it is in a confined space. What do you think?" he asked the others.

"Um I'm not sure that would work" said Verity thoughtfully. "Wouldn't he see us first?"

"Don't you think it would be better if one, or perhaps two of us went on ahead of him?" suggested Rupert. "Then we could block his path, both in front and behind him and there would be less chance of him escaping from us even if he did see us."

The others looked at him in astonishment.

"Gosh, what a good idea." replied Verity, sounding very impressed and wishing she had thought of that idea first.

"I think you and I should be the ones to try to get ahead of him." added Bradley looking at Pythagorus as he spoke.

"I agree," said Francois "you two are always chasing each other on your seahorses and you are much faster than the rest of us." The others nodded their heads in agreement.

"I agree but I think you should go separately." added Verity. "One to the left and one to the right, and then hopefully, at least one of you will get in front of Peter without being seen. You will have to ride quite a distance around him, to make sure that he doesn't become suspicious or recognise either of you." She added, sounding rather worried, as she understood the enormity of the situation they were in. "Say a nautical mile either side?"

"Don't worry about that." replied Bradley trying to reassure her. "We'll soon get around him. After all he's not riding very fast at the moment, and we are both very, very fast when we want to be!"

"True." agreed Verity, not sounding very convinced.

"Don't worry about them Verity." added Sophia. "They really are much faster than any of us and we think they are going to win the seahorse races at the end of term."

"Shall I meet you at the entrance to the second tunnel in say half an hour?" Pythagorus asked Bradley, looking at his watch.

"No problem," agreed Bradley, "I'll go left and you can go right, and I bet I beat you there!" he added grinning mischievously.

"No way," responded Pythagorus accepting the challenge. "you know that I can easily beat you!"

"Now, now you two." intervened Verity shaking her finger at them. "Don't forget that you must firstly make sure that Peter doesn't see you and secondly you must beat him to the tunnels. These are both much more important than seeing who gets there first! Please, please be careful." she added.

"Of course we will." they both responded apologetically.

"Sorry we were only trying to encourage each other to ride fast" Pythagorus explained.

"Now stop worrying all of you," added Bradley confidently "and we will see you shortly in the tunnels". Then turning to Pythagorus he called "Ready Pythagorus" and then he counted: "one, two three...," and they both set off as fast as they could in opposite directions before the others could stop them or even wish them good luck.

Verity sighed as they watched them go. "I hope they know what they are doing!"

"Don't worry," replied Francois, "honestly they are very, very fast, and if anyone can beat Peter to the tunnels it's those two!"

Neptune, Newton and the others had by this time finally reached their first destination, which was the entrance to the gold mines. The gold mines were located in the middle of a group of hills, which seemed to rise up out of the seabed from nowhere. The entrance to the mines was blocked by two enormous black cast iron doors, which kept out the seawater.

The doors themselves were about 20 feet high and two large growling lions were etched into the middle of each door. The lions were so lifelike; they looked like they were about to jump out of the doors which made some of them feel a little nervous when they looked up at them.

The actual entrance to the mines was through a much smaller door cut out of the bottom of one of the cast iron doors, which then lead into a vacuumed chamber. Although there were many mines within the hills this was the only entrance. The mines were all connected either by underground tunnels or glycon shafts leading across the seabed floor towards the mines on the next hill rather than running deep into the ground.

There were many different types of mines stretching over many miles either under the ground or in the hills and they were full of many precious metals and stones including gold, diamonds and rubies. To save time, the Atlantians had built a rail track across their complete length, which twisted and turned as it ran up and down through the tunnels and shafts. They had then built trains that looked similar to trams which carried both the workers and the precious metals in and out of the mines.

As it was Sunday, the mines were closed for the day and the heavy machines used to unearth the precious stones and metals were silent. There was no sign of any trains moving along the tracks, however the lights in the shafts and tunnels were still lit and there were lights gleaming on top of the hills. These lights were kept on at all times to prevent any accidents. Not all eels had such a good sense of direction as Ellie and in the early years, one of them had accidentally knocked one of the glycon shafts over and caused a lot of damage and some serious flooding. With the mines silent and still and the lights flickering in the distance through the water it was quite an eerie place to be on your own.

When they finally arrived at the doors, they were not at all surprised to find that Neptune knew the password needed for the key lock to open the small door, and within a few minutes they were inside the main entrance room to the mines. Courtney was feeling pretty scared by this time and clung onto to Eugene's arm in the same way that a limpet clings to rocks. But Eugene took pity on her realising how scared she was and squeezed her hand to give her reassurance and she responded with a rather watery smile.

Neptune checked the room carefully and seemed to sniff the air before leading them through a couple of small rooms until they found themselves in a vast, tall chamber, which to their amazement contained both a train station and a garage. The garage was filled with row upon row of trains, all of which were ready and waiting for their next trip. They were all individually painted in various colours and some had brightly coloured faces painted on the front of their engines. Each one looked different and on closer inspection had different names.

"Right" said Neptune looking at them all thoughtfully "the only way I can think of to establish whether Mr Magnihyde has come this way, is to count the number of trains here in the garage. Then we will know if he is using one to escape"

The others looked at him aghast.

"But there must be hundreds of trains here" said Courtney looking at the large number of rows of trains in front of her.

"737 to be precise." Neptune informed them.

"Right, I suggest we split up into pairs. Eugene and Newton, you walk over to the far left corner and start counting them from that end. Courtney and I will count them from this end and when we meet in the middle we will add the two numbers together. Now off you run," he added "as we don't have much time."

The two boys ran to the other end of the garage and began to count. The counting seemed to take hours, but in fact it was only about 10 minutes before they all met up in the middle.

"We make it 393." said Neptune. "How many have you counted?"

"340." replied Eugene.

"Oh dear," responded Neptune gloomily, "that only makes 733. We will have to count them again!"

"I wish Pythagorus was here." muttered Newton as they turned their backs on each other and began counting again, but this time in the opposite direction. "He's much better at maths than me!"

"Shush," interrupted Eugene glaring at him. "I can't concentrate when you are talking."

This time, the counting took them about fifteen minutes as they were much more methodical in their counting.

"345" yelled Eugene to Neptune from the other end of the garage when they had finished counting the trains again.

"392" replied Neptune. "That's 737 trains which means that Mr Magnihyde can't have come this way.

Their voices echoed around the chamber as they spoke, but in the middle of the echo they heard a loud bang, like the sound of a metal door slamming shut, and then a strange whooshing noise that they couldn't identify.

"Do you think that was Mr Magnihyde?" Courtney whispered to Neptune anxiously.

But Neptune didn't respond. Instead, he yelled up to the boys at the end of the garage to run back towards the entrance as fast as they could which instinctively they had already started doing as soon as they heard the noise. The four of them quickly headed back to the main entrance and the outer door which unfortunately was in the same direction as the mysterious noise. As they ran, in front of them they could see a small trickle of water heading towards them, which turned into a running stream by the time they reached the main entrance room.

Chapter 20

When they reached the entrance, to their horror, they found themselves looking through a small perfectly round hole in the middle of one of the main doors. Water was gushing through the hole directly into the room, and as they stared at it in shock, it started to grow bigger and bigger. It was a very odd hole in that it was a perfect circle.

It was as if someone had taken a huge apple corer and used it to bore a hole in the door. The water was by now gushing in so fiercely, with all the water in Oceana trying to push through the hole. They couldn't wade through it to reach the door and the entrance room was quickly filling up with water.

Neptune had visibly paled when he initially saw the hole in the door and momentarily seemed to freeze, but luckily not for long. Although he wasn't as good a magician as Artimas, he was still a grandmaster and he immediately recognised the powerful magic that had been used to create the hole. Newton found that he couldn't stop shivering as he sensed the intensity of the evil in the magic and felt some left over particles which were still bouncing around the room. Mr Magnihyde was obviously much more than a simple laboratory assistant!

"Come to me quickly." Neptune commanded them holding out his hands towards them. "We must make up a magic circle."

"We need to hold hands and stand in a circle." he continued. "Now close your eyes and concentrate and imagine that the circle in the door is now in the middle of us. Now I want you to imagine yourselves holding the circle in your hands and squeezing the hole shut. Do you understand?" he asked them anxiously.

They all nodded their heads and a few seconds passed, which to them felt like hours as they all did as they were told and concentrated on closing up the hole. Courtney felt a little bit silly standing holding hands in a circle, even if she was holding Eugene's hand! She opened her eyes a little and peeped at him, only to hear Neptune telling her off and commanding her to obey him immediately. Just before she did, she quickly glanced at the hole, which was still growing larger and larger, despite what they were trying to do.

The water was now lapping at her heels. It was obviously not working. Perhaps, she thought guiltily, she had better start concentrating!

This time when Neptune instructed them to keep squeezing the hole they were all concentrating very hard. It slowly started to close and they immediately became aware of a warm glow gradually coming up through their hands. What they couldn't see because their eyes were all closed, was the orange light that had suddenly shot out from the middle of their hands to form a ring of light immediately above them and in the middle of the circle they had created.

The ring of light was the exact same size of the hole in the door and as they squeezed the hole in their minds, the orange ring in front of them started to grow smaller and the hole in the door also stopped growing and began to shrink in a similar way.

Within a couple of minutes the whole process was completed. The ring of light became a single ray and then disappeared, and the hole both in their minds and the door were squeezed shut. As the hole closed, the whooshing sound stopped just as suddenly as it had started and the warm glow in their hands ebbed away. They finally opened their eyes and to their relief the hole in the door was gone and it seemed that the crisis was over. Neptune sank down

134

to the floor in exhaustion forgetting all about the pool of water on the floor and unfortunately getting very wet in the process.

"Where did the hole come from and how did we manage to get rid of it?" asked a very mystified Courtney a few minutes later.

"My guess" responded Eugene, "is that Mr Magnihyde somehow saw us enter the mines and he created the hole to try and kill us and stop us from preventing him leave Oceana."

Neptune nodded his head in agreement, still too exhausted to speak. Newton who was feeling a little dizzy from the left over vibes of the magic Mr Magnihyde had used, asked Neptune if this meant that Mr Magnihyde was also a grandmaster as surely not many people could create such a hole. Neptune nodded his head in agreement but as far as he knew he was not.

"I agree Mr Magnihyde must know that we are looking for him otherwise he wouldn't have bothered to create the hole when he saw us come into the mines." Eugene suddenly suggested thoughtfully. "Do you think this means he also knows about the ancient door?"

"Quite possibly." replied Neptune who was now starting to recover back his energy. Then he suddenly sat up and added excitedly, "But what he might have forgotten, or perhaps he didn't know, is that after you have created such a powerful spell, it take hours for your own aura to recover its energy."

"Our energy comes from the minerals in the water and as your aura extracts the minerals it needs, it expels those that it doesn't need. As a result, it produces a chemical reaction with the water, which in turn colours the water pink. We should be able to find him by following his trail, but," he added, "we only have a few hours because after that he will have fully recovered and all traces of him will be lost."

"He obviously doesn't think we will come out of this alive," responded Eugene thoughtfully, "so he won't be trying to cover his tracks."

"I agree." Neptune replied. Then looking at Newton and smiling he added "That's because he didn't realise we had Newton with us, and thankfully he must be unaware of his natural powers, which are very rare, and enabled us to defeat his magic. Come," he added getting up, "there is not much time to lose. We must go after him. Let's just hope the animals had the sense to hide when they heard him coming."

The four of them then wadded their way to the entrance door and headed back outside. To their relief, the animals were waiting for them anxiously and they rushed up to them in delight, as they had thought they were all dead! The miners, they decided were certainly in for a huge shock when they next came back to work as the whole of the main entrance room floor was covered in water.

They set off, following the tiny pink trail of bubbles that Mr Magnihyde had left which seemed to lead them back in the general direction of the pearl factories, but which disappeared after about half an hours riding. This was much sooner than they had expected but they decided however to carry on in this direction, as the pearl factories were where Newton thought the secret door was located and there was nothing else nearby that could be of interest.

Whilst Newton and the others had been trapped in the mines, Pythagorus and Bradley had raced Goldie and Pegasus as fast as they could in a huge arc around Peter. As agreed, they had ridden about a mile to each side of him, before racing ahead towards the entrance to the tunnels. Neither of them had to direct their seahorses, as they both seem to know where they were going and when to change direction. Amazingly, when you took into account the distance they had just travelled, they arrived at the entrance at exactly the same time! They were both exhausted and their seahorses were breathing very deeply, but it had been a lot of fun.

They rode cautiously up the tunnel together towards the second tunnel and they were pleased to see that there were no signs of Peter anywhere. They had obviously beaten him.

At the end of the first tunnel were a couple of chambers leading into the second tunnel. The outer chamber contained the sentry boxes whereas the inner chamber was much smaller with soft lighting and was obviously used as a meeting place. They hadn't really studied this chamber when they had first arrived in Oceana, but as they looked around now, they noticed that there were a couple of tables and chairs scattered around the room. A big terracotta pot placed on each side of the chamber, contained a couple of large potted plants, and gave the chamber a garden terrace sort of feeling. They decided to hide behind one of the pots, but as there wasn't much room, they had to separate and so they hid themselves behind both of the pots.

Thank heavens, they thought, for the dim lighting!

Pythagorus stroked the dagger in his belt hoping that we would not need to use it.

Rupert, Francois and Sofia meanwhile sat tight on Ellie's back and together with Verity continued to follow Peter, but as they approached the entrance to the tunnels she quickened her pace until they were only about 50 paces behind him. Luckily for them, Peter so was engrossed with riding his own seahorse and the efforts required to keep hold of all of his luggage, he didn't see them!

Some of his luggage was now trailing behind him in the water, tied to his seahorse with long pieces of string. Other pieces were bound together with leather straps and he held these straps tightly in his hand. He looked like he was carrying all of his worldly goods with him and it was no wonder, they thought, that he was travelling so slowly. It also explained why he was so oblivious to them following him. Peter obviously had no idea that Newton had seen him leave Artimas' room.

Peter entered the first tunnel and began the final leg of his journey out of Oceana. As he reached about half way along the tunnel he suddenly became aware of some movement from the waves created by Ellie as she swam in the water behind him, and when he idly turned around to see who else was travelling back to the upper world, he was shocked to see the grim faces of Francois, Sofia, Rupert, Verity and Ellie following only a few yards behind.

Chapter 21

At this point it suddenly dawned on Peter that Newton might have seen him after all, and as he started to panic, he urged his seahorse to quicken his pace in a desperate attempt to escape them. In his hurry, he leant forward and grabbed hold of his seahorse's reins and in the process accidentally let go of some of the straps he was holding. The four friends found themselves being bombarded with pieces of floating luggage.

Luckily, nothing actually hit them but the loss of the luggage enabled Peter to speed up. He raced towards the second tunnel with Ellie, who was now dodging the floating luggage, chasing behind him but she couldn't catch him up.

Peter, of course hadn't bargained for Pythagorus and Bradley lying in wait for him. As he entered the first chamber he was still looking behind him rather than in front, laughing at Ellie's desperate attempt to catch him. So he didn't see the boys leap out from their hiding places when they saw him enter the chamber, or dash in front of him to block his path.

In fact the first time he became aware of them was when his seahorse suddenly performed an emergency stop in order to avoid a collision with the other seahorses. He went sailing over his seahorse's head, landing head first on the floor at Pythagorus and Bradley's feet, with a couple of his bags raining down on top of him.

Looking desperate he jumped up and staggered forwards, flinging his bags aside and sending clothes and books everywhere as some of the bags burst open.

He started to make a run for the second chamber, but he was too late. Rupert, Francois and Sofia had already jumped off Ellie's back and together with Pythagorus, Verity, Bradley and the seahorses they all surrounded him and blocked him from escaping. Many pairs of hands grabbed him as Verity threw the rope that Jock had given them around his body and pulled it tight.

He was trapped and they all cheered and hugged each other in delight. All except Peter that is!!

For the next half hour they tried to interrogate Peter, but he refused to say a word and just sat there and sulked. They also searched both him and his bags but there was no sign of the ruby. So Pythagorus and Bradley, who were the strongest lifted him up and put him across Ellie's back with his hands still firmly tied behind his back. Sofia then tied one of her silk scarves around his mouth to stop him from screaming out but she complained bitterly about having to use one of her best scarves.

In the meantime Rupert, Verity and Francois collected up all the bags and clothes scattered across the chamber and also piled them onto Ellie's back. Once all of his things were tied to her back, there was only just about enough room for two of them to ride between her two humps so Rupert rode Peter's seahorse instead.

Ellie's load was very heavy now and thankfully, it was lucky she was so strong as she soon managed to start swimming again.

They then set off for the long journey back to school. Once outside the tunnel and back in the waters out of anyone else's earshot, Pythagorus called his brother up on the phone to give him the great news of Peter's capture. He was feeling rather concerned about Newton as whilst they were hiding in the chamber waiting for Peter to arrive he had suddenly felt very wet and cold. A few seconds later he had felt very hot. An image of a red circle, which had just appeared from out of nowhere, seemed to shrink and then disappear in his mind and for some strange reason he now felt very weak and exhausted.

It was very odd, but all the time this was happening, some sixth sense had told him that these thoughts were actually Newton's thoughts and that his brother was in some sort of danger. He couldn't of course find out until Peter was captured and they were back in the water, so it was with some anxiety that he called him and he felt an immense relief when he heard the sound of Newton's voice on the other end of the phone.

He was safe after all!

The two of then chatted for a few minutes and updated each other with their news.

"We've just caught Peter," Pythagorus whispered to his brother excitedly, "but he won't talk to us, so we are taking him back to Artimas so that he can force him to talk. It was very exciting and Bradley and I had to race around him, but we both arrived at the tunnels together. There's no sign of Mr Magnihyde yet. Are you all right by the way?" he added "I had some really weird thoughts about a red circle, and I felt very wet and cold and then very hot."

Pythagoras's words all came out in a hurried jumble of words – it was a good job his brother understood him!

"Wow," responded Newton equally excited "everyone says well done."

"We're heading for the pearl factories now, but we think Mr Magnihyde just tried to kill us in the mines." he continued. "Someone made a magic hole appear in the front door, which was letting in all of the water and we could have drowned. That red circle you saw sounds like the one we created in our minds in order to close up the hole."

141

"Isn't it amazing that you saw it too!" he carried on speaking very quickly into the phone."

Neptune says that you are to hurry back to the school and get Peter to Artimas so that he can interrogate him and find out everything he knows about Mr Magnihyde, why he stole the ruby, and where he is heading. I guess you haven't found the ruby yet?" he finished.

"No. I'm afraid not." Pythagorus responded. "Be careful Newton and as soon as we've taken Peter to Artimas, we'll come and join you at the pearl factories."

"Wait for us there" he continued "but I'll let you know if there is any further news before then. See you later." he added and rang off before his brother could respond, feeling much happier now that he knew Newton was safe.

Pythagorus then told the others what had happened and they were all quite shocked when they heard of the narrow escape in the mines, and they were of course very relieved that everyone was safe and unharmed. After chatting for a while they decided that Mr Magnihyde was probably the one carrying the ruby and not Peter.

Pythagorus and the others sped off back towards school as fast as they could. However, Ellie and the other seahorses were getting quite tired and thirsty by now as they had not stopped for a few hours, and Peter's bags were amazingly heavy. He was obviously carrying the kitchen sink! So they were delighted when about an hour later they saw Jock, Archie, some other sixth formers and some spare seahorses arriving in the distance. They had followed the silvery trail that Ellie had left behind her in the water and had easily found them.

As they swapped news, the sixth formers gave Ellie and the seahorses some very welcome food and water that they had brought with them. Anyone seeing them would have thought they were having a picnic! Jock also tried to interrogate Peter, but although he spoke to him very sharply, Peter turned his head away from him and refused to speak a word. Jock was very disappointed.

It was soon agreed that the best plan would be if they split up again. Some of the sixth formers would take charge of Peter and his belongings and they soon bundled them all onto the spare seahorses. They had offered their own seahorses to Pythagorus and Bradley, but Pegasus, Goldie and the others did not want to leave their masters, as they felt surprisingly refreshed after some food and a short rest.

Ellie also felt much better now that Peter and his bags had been taken away, as her load was now much lighter. She was quite happy to swop him for the extra food and water for Newton and the others. Verity now had her seahorse Genevieve so she was also feeling much happier.

Jock, Archie and two of the sixth formers Hugo and Tatiana joined Pythagorus and the others, and they turned around and headed off towards the pearl factories, to see if they could help Newton and the others capture Mr Magnihyde.

As they swam along, Pythagorus updated Jock on what had happened to Newton and the others in the mines, and Jock was very shocked by the news. He urged them all to go as fast as they could to catch the others up. The other sixth formers led by Stefan meanwhile set off back towards school and specifically Artimas' office so that they could pass Peter to him and update him on what had happened.

When the sixth formers got back to school a few hours later, they soon found out that Artimas was recovering very well from his injuries. They took Peter up to his office, and when Artimas saw him he flew into a terrible rage. He started dancing around shouting and waving his staff in the air, which in turn sent off magic sparks flying around the room some of which hit Peter on the head. Peter meanwhile was crouching on the floor with his hands over his head, shaking.

The sixth formers cowered in the corner of the room in fright even though they knew that the rage and magic was not aimed at them. No one had ever seen Artimas this angry before and it was quite a sight to behold.

Artimas was in fact making such a commotion that matron came rushing over from her room to see what was happening, thinking that he was being attacked again. When she saw him flying around the room in such a rage, she scolded him very badly. It was only then, that Artimas started to calm down and Stefan was finally able to tell him that although Pythagorus and the others had found Peter, there was no sign of Mr Magnihyde, and although they had searched all of his bags, there was no sign of the ruby.

Jock, Pythagorus and some of the others, Stefan explained, had set off to help Newton and the others find Mr Magnihyde, and he then told him what had happened to them in the mines. Artimas became very angry again when he heard this news but this time he managed to control his temper and remained calmer. They could however tell that he was still very cross as the odd spark still flew out of his staff behind him.

"Where is the ruby Peter?" demanded Artimas after he had heard all of the news, angrily circling him.

"Why did you steal the ruby from me?" he snapped.

"What is Magnihyde going to do with it?" he added.

"Where has he gone?" he continued angrily.

Chapter 22

Artimas inundated Peter with question after question but Peter refused to answer him or even look at him. Once the initial anger had worn off, Artimas tried everything from warmth to coldness, shaking, bribing and even pleading to try to extract information from him - he even threatened to turn him into a lizard, but absolutely nothing worked. All Peter would do was shake his head and say that he was truly sorry that he had hurt him, but even then he didn't sound very convincing!

After about an hour of constant questioning and just as they were about to give up, Peter finally broke down sobbing and admitted that Mr Magnihyde had forced him to steal the ruby by blackmailing him and the full story then came tumbling out.

But this was only after Artimas had threatened to cast a truthfulness spell on Peter (which makes you spit out frogs when you speak for weeks afterwards) and he had explained to him that if the ruby disappeared into the upper world then Oceana and the school would be flooded and everything would be lost forever. All of them including Peter, he told him would die.

"I'm very, very sorry Artimas" Peter said, sobbing uncontrollably. "But he made me steal the ruby."

"How?" Artimas demanded.

"He.. He found out that I had been in prison in the upper world for assault." he stammered nervously. "When I was about 18, I got drunk one day and I got into a silly fight and I accidentally pushed this lad through a window and he ended up in hospital with a broken leg and cracked ribs. I didn't mean to hurt him, but they didn't believe me so I was charged with assault, and they sentenced me to two years in prison. I've never drunk again since that day."

"Anyway" he continued "Mr Magnihyde had seen the reports in the papers in the upper world and he recognised me when I arrived at the school, and he threatened to tell you and get me sacked if I didn't steal the ruby for him."

"I didn't have any choice." he added miserably. "And I really loved it here."

"Keep talking." Artimas told him grimly.

"Well after I stole the ruby from you I met up with him at the Coral Café in town and that's when I gave him the ruby. He never told me where he was going or what he was going to do with it, and I didn't know that it was so special. We then both left and I set off back towards the upper world and Pythagorus and some others caught me in the tunnels."

"I didn't think Newton had seen me." he added sounded a little sulky.

"And that's it?" Artimas asked him sounding very exasperated.

"Yes." Peter replied sounding very unsure and a little scared.

"So what is this?" Artimas demanded shoving a blank piece of paper in front of Peter's nose, which he had previously found in one of his pockets.

"Just a, a, a piece of paper." stuttered Peter even more nervously.

"Huh!" Artimas responded angrily.

146

Artimas walked to his desk, laid the piece of paper carefully down and straightened up some of the creases. He then picked up a small green bottle from his cabinet and sprinkled a few drops of the lime green water onto the paper.

A few seconds later, the paper turned blue, and it quickly became covered in lines and then words to reveal a cheque in Peter's name which was signed by Mr Magnihyde for £100,000.

Everyone in the room gasped in shock when they saw both the cheque and the amount appear. If he was prepared to pay Peter this much they thought, how much was the ruby itself worth?

Peter looked down at the floor, too ashamed to look at them. "Everything I told you is true." he stammered, "That was just a bonus if I managed to steal the ruby for him."

"Honestly." he added nervously, looking at Artimas, as if pleading with him to believe him.

Artimas sank down shocked into his chair, and sighed sadly. His worst fears were happening. The ruby had been stolen deliberately.

"But don't you know you can't take the ruby out of Oceana?" Artimas told him angrily" "it will just disintegrate and our magic powers will be lost forever."

"Take Peter away and lock him downstairs in the cellars whilst I decide what to do with him." he commanded coldly. "Make sure he is guarded at all times."

Once they had gone, Artimas picked up the phone and firstly called Jock to tell him everything that Peter had told him and the fact that the ruby was still missing. Jock in turn updated Artimas on what he understood had actually happened in the mines and Artimas again became very angry but also very fearful when he heard how close some of them had been to being killed.

"Where are you now and where are the others?" he asked Jock.

"We are about an hour past the city walls and I reckon we are about two hours away from the pearl factories and the others." Jock told him. "We may even arrive before them, but we should be a strong team once we are all together."

"I think you will need all of Neptune's powers and all of your strength to overcome him. I wish I could be with you," Artimas added, "but first I must make some calls and try and see if there is anything we can do to protect ourselves just in case you don't manage to find the ruby."

"Please be careful and call me as soon as there is some news. The whole of Oceana's future lies in your hands." he added wearily.

"Don't worry," Jock told him confidently, "we will find him and we will get the ruby back."

Artimas then tried to call Neptune but there was no answer. Either Neptune had turned off his phone he thought or something had happened to them.

Fearing the worst, Artimas then had the unenviable task of contacting the King of Oceana, Prince Henry, to explain the perilous situation they were now facing. Prince Henry took it very badly, and ranted and raved at Artimas for nearly 10 minutes before he finally started to calm down and allowed Artimas to tell him everything that had happened to them all.

When he realised that Artimas had actually been hurt in the attack he spent the next 5 minutes checking that he was really OK, before allowing Artimas to relay the rest of the story. As you can imagine, he was even more dismayed when he heard about the events in the mines.

It was only when Artimas was describing Mr Magnihyde to him, of his love for Country and Western music and his unusual habit of wearing cowboy boots that Prince Henry gasped in shock. He suddenly remembered a Chancellor that his father, Prince Frederick had employed a number of years ago.

"Don't you remember him?" Prince Henry asked Artimas" He was a distant cousin of ours called Lord Solumun. He was very, very bright and he became one of the youngest grand masters of his time. He was once tipped to take over as headmaster of the school from your predecessor."

"I remember hearing his name mentioned as a child but people always stopped talking about him when they saw me arrive." Artimas explained.

"Well," Prince Henry continued, "one day my father caught him stealing some of the gold from the mines, which he was selling directly to the upper world. He was amassing a large fortune for himself rather than ploughing it back into Oceana. He was also paying all the miners a lower salary than we had agreed, and was keeping the extra monies for himself."

When my father discovered this" he added "they had a huge row and father stripped him of all his titles and took away his chain of office. Father managed to retrieve back most of the gold and wealth he had stolen, and he paid the miners a huge bonus to compensate for all of the monies Solumun had taken from them."

"I remember the bonus." Artimas interrupted. "That was talked about for years afterwards. No one could ever figure out why it had been such a bumper year."

"Well Father thought it was better to pay them a bonus than tell them all the truth." Prince Henry explained. "He also gave them all a large pay rise."

"I remember that too." Artimas said interrupting Prince Henry again.

"Father then banished him and the rest of his family to exile in the upper world." Prince Henry then continued. "If I remember correctly, but I was only about 5 years old at the time."

"Solumun had a son called Magnius, who must have been about 10 years old when they left. I'm sure he had a passion even then for Country music and American cowboys and especially cowboy boots. Do you remember any of this Artimas?" he asked.

"Yes, I do remember hearing tales about someone being exiled when I was younger, but I must admit I had forgotten all about it." Artimas told him thoughtfully. "Solumun must have taught his son everything he knew about magic and life in Oceana, which is why he had so much knowledge of the ruby and its powers, and why he can perform such sophisticated magic." he added.

"Solumun and Magnius are obviously seeking revenge for my father's actions by trying to destroy our kingdom." added Prince Henry anxiously. "We must do everything in our power to stop them."

"Newton is a very gifted child," Artimas told him "and with his brother's strength, for he is not strong enough without him, and Neptune's knowledge and powers, I am sure they will be able to stop Magnius from taking the ruby into the upper lands. I will follow them as soon as I feel stronger." he finished.

"No, no." responded Prince Henry firmly. "You must stay in the school and preserve all of your strength in case Magnius is successful in taking the ruby. We will need all of your powers to hold up the roof long enough for the people to escape. I will tell my father and the rest of my family the terrible news and when the time comes we will get ready to help you."

"In the meantime," he told him, "you must contact Neptune and tell him precisely who he is dealing with. Let me know as soon as you hear any further news." he added and rang off.

At this point, matron bustled into Artimas' room bringing in with her the doctor and a nice strong cup of tea with a dash of honey for him, as she was still very concerned over his injuries, especially after his fit of temper! The doctor immediately began examining him, whilst matron continued to fuss over him, so he didn't have an opportunity to try to phone Neptune again or the others to warn them how dangerous Magnius could be.

By the time they finally left him alone, he was too late, as Neptune had already ordered them all to turn off their phones. So he telephoned Mr Pinkleton instead. Mr Pinkleton was also a grandmaster and Artimas needed some of his magic potions. He also wanted someone to talk to.

Chapter 23

As both Jock and Artimas had anticipated, Pythagorus, Newton and their respective groups arrived at the entrance to the channel leading to the pearl factories within a few minutes of each other. The twins and the Octets were reunited again. With Neptune, Jock, Eugene, Verity, Hugo and the other sixth formers, they made up a group of about sixteen.

Quite a formidable team when you took into account both the magical powers and the determination they had between them, and not forgetting of course, the animals!

To arrive at the pearl factories, you had to first travel through an immense stretch of nothing but water, which had obviously once been a great ocean. You then passed by some small islands, which were edged with pretty coves and sandy beaches. Despite being under water the islands were covered in palm trees, which had somehow survived the flooding and had adapted to their new surroundings. If you closed your eyes tight, you could almost see the sails of a pirate ship, hiding in waiting in one of the coves for an unsuspecting ship to travel past their way.

Now, some of the islands were used as summer camps for the villagers and you could just see some tents if you looked carefully through the trees. A little further on, you passed through a narrow channel in-between two small, but very tall mountainous islands, which were sitting very close together. This channel led you to a large set of doors and then directly into the pearl factories.

Travelling through this channel could be a very hazardous journey to undertake, because on the bottom of the sea floor lay a reef which could tear you to pieces if you accidentally touched it. The walls of the channel, which were very steep and impossible to climb, went up nearly as high as the roof itself so it was a very dark and dangerous place to be, especially for people who did not know their way.

It was also deathly quiet, as being a Sunday, there were no other animals or people for miles around them. They were all at home oblivious to the imminent danger facing them all!

Luckily for them, Ellie knew this route very well. Twice a week she was employed as a taxi to take some of the supervisors into the pearl factories for their daily shift. Rather than waiting around for the shift to end doing nothing, she would sometimes carry boxes of pearls, packed inside one of her carriages, to some waiting barges located on one of the nearby islands. Once full, these barges were then pulled by one of the dozen whales still living in Oceana towards smaller goods tunnels located nearby.

Through the use of an elaborate pulley system, these goods tunnels were used to transport the boxes of pearls up to the upper world. The tunnels were very tall and narrow and covered in slimy seaweed so it would be impossible for anyone to use them to escape back to the upper world.

In return for their day's work, Ellie and the other electric eels and whales were allowed to live freely in Oceana. Their wages were fresh fish caught daily from the Atlantic Ocean, which were transported back down for them to eat using the same pulley system and goods tunnels. So everyone was happy!

After they had all rested for a while and eaten and drunk some of the food and water Jock and the others had brought with them, Ellie led them slowly and carefully along the narrow channel, and the others followed behind on their seahorses. Neptune on Pluto and Jock on his seahorse Aldanti, followed at the rear talking quietly about recent events and trying to decide how they were going to best approach the task ahead.

They were about half way along the channel, when there was a sudden commotion in the front followed by a scream. Archie who was riding on Ellie and who still had mild concussion had been leaning back talking to Sofia about the earlier incident in the pool with the hockey stick. Unfortunately he had leant back too far, slipped off Ellie's back and had fallen head first towards the reef. He was not having a good day!

Sofia had managed to grab hold of one of his legs as he fell but his weight had also pulled her off Ellie's back. Luckily, Rupert who was riding next to them had just managed to grab one of her arms in time, which thankfully had stopped the pair from falling down onto the reef itself.

They were however now hanging precariously only inches away from the tips of the reef itself and Rupert was struggling to keep hold of them. Ellie swimming backwards managed to grab hold of Archie's top in her mouth and quickly swam upwards and away from the immediate danger pulling them all behind her.

Francois who was also close by leaned forward to help Rupert keep hold of Sofia, whilst Eugene and Hugo swam up under Ellie and thankfully were able to hoist both Archie and Sofia back on to Ellie's back, without too many problems. Archie and Sofia were then fussed over by the others for a few minutes, checking to see if they had been hurt by the reef.

It had been yet another close shave!

Whilst everyone was sorting themselves out and once they knew that no one was hurt, Newton and Pythagorus wandered past them a little, curious to see what was

154

ahead as they could see a glimmer of light in the distance. As they rode towards the light they suddenly heard their Uncle shout "Stop" in such a commanding voice that they instantly did as they were told, and their seahorses immediately stood still and trod water. Artimas and Jock dashed up towards them and stopped just a few inches behind them.

"Don't move forward even an inch." Neptune commanded Goldie and Koi. The seahorses nodded their heads and remained motionless whilst he rummaged through his rucksack, grabbed hold of one of the sea snails and threw it into the channel in front of them.

It sailed just a few inches past Pythagorus' nose, and then suddenly there was an almighty bang and the water in the channel was lit up with a dazzling white and blue light, as an electric impulse shot past them through the water and hit some of the rocks on either side of them. I'm afraid to say that the sea snail was burnt instantly. Newton realised with a gulp that they had been only inches away from instant death as neither of them had seen anything unusual in the water ahead of them.

But the danger was still not over. Just as they were thinking how lucky they had been not to swim into the electric force field, the rocks above them started to tremble and they could hear a strange cracking noise above their heads.

"Oh no!" Jock exclaimed to Neptune looking up at the walls in disbelief. "It looks like there is going to be a landslide."

"You're right." responded Neptune. "Quick, we must get out of here before we are buried under the rocks. Hurry everyone." he added urgently, beckoning them all to follow him as quickly as they could.

He then spurred Pluto to swim as fast as he could upwards and out of the channel, and with the others following closely behind him, they sped off. Behind them, they heard another strange cracking noise and then the sounds of rocks falling and splashing down in the water with an almighty bang, creating a tidal wave in their wake. They only just managed to reach the end of the channel, and pass through the door before a huge boulder from one of the two walls fell into the water, knocking over the door and blocking the entrance to the channel.

At the same time, the tidal wave swept over them, the force of it knocking Neptune, Bradley and Newton off their seahorses, sending them crashing to the floor. Luckily, the floor bed just the other side of the channel was made of sand and they did not hurt themselves when they hit the ground. When they looked behind them, they could see no sign of the channel having ever existed, just a wall of rocks, a cloud of dust and a strange burning smell in the water.

"How did you know something was in the water in front of us Neptune?" Pythagorus asked as he helped his brother get back up from the floor. They others jumped off their seahorses and stretched their legs for a few minutes whilst occasionally gazing up at the cliffs behind them, as they contemplated how lucky they'd been.

"Yes, what an earth was that Neptune?" asked Jock who was as equally shocked as the children. Even though he was an Atlantian by birth, he had not had much formal magic training. It had been immediately apparent at school, that much like Bradley, riding seahorses was where his skills lay. The Atlantians believed that seahorses were sacred and their training was nearly as important as magic, so he had been encouraged to dedicate his life to both looking after and training them.

"Mr Magnihyde obviously came this way at some stage and set a trap." responded Neptune, looking around them cautiously as he spoke, checking to see that he wasn't hiding somewhere close to them, listening in on their conversation.

"It was an electrically charged force field which was invisible to the naked eye. He would have needed to extract the electricity directly from an electric eel to create such a force field as that amount of charge is certainly not something you can buy from Mr Pinkleton's shop." he added thoughtfully.

"Yes but how did you spot it Neptune?" Bradley asked him, still brushing the sand off his tracksuit.

"Well as Goldie and Koi approached the force field," he explained, "they created a small ripple in the water around them, some of which swept in front of them and touched the fence. The weight of the ripple forced it to move slightly, and as it moved I caught sight of a shimmer of light in the water, and I heard the faint tinkling sound of the ripple splashing against its surface."

"It was lucky" he added "that I was looking ahead at that point, and not at Archie's foolishness."

"I'm very sorry Neptune," responded Archie in a very small voice looking down at the ground as he spoke "I promise I will be more careful in the future."

"I should think so." responded Neptune not quite as sternly as he sounded. "Now we have wasted enough time here. Have a quick drink all of you, then we must press on quickly but very carefully. I have a feeling that the force field is not the only trap Mr Magnihyde has set for us. The only question is, did he set the trap at some point over the weekend, or just as he was escaping. Now all of you, and that includes you Ellie and all of you seahorses, keep your

157

eyes and ears open and tell me the second you see or feel anything suspicious."

Whilst Neptune had been talking to them, Ellie swam a bit further round the bottom of the sheer cliff which edged one of the mountainous islands. She suddenly let out a high pitched squeal. There, lying on one of the lower rocks was one of her electric eel friends, Daphne, who was looking very poorly.

Her black velvet skin no longer glistened and looked damp and dull and she was shivering with cold. Her eyes were yellow rather than the normal bright red, although it was difficult to see them as she lay there moaning and her eyes were half closed. Instead of the normal smile, her mouth was pinched and taut and she was obviously in a lot of pain. When she heard the sound of Ellie's voice a big tear slipped down the side of her cheek and fell onto the ground but she didn't move.

"Don't worry Ellie." said Neptune gently as he bent down to examine Daphne. "We can soon sort her out, but I'm afraid that I'm going to have to take some of your electricity to make her better as she won't survive the trip back to the school. Do you think you can cope with that Ellie?"

Ellie nodded her head, tears welling up in her eyes as she looked down at her friend. She hated injections but she would do anything to help her friend.

So she turned herself around carefully so as not to create too many waves in the water and gingerly lifted up her tail. Francois, Verity, Sofia and Courtney hugged her neck tightly to give her some moral support as Neptune took out some scissors and a needle from his haversack. It was always fascinating to see what things he stored in his haversack!

He carefully cut a small hole in the tip of Ellie's tail and using the needle, extracted a small amount of her blood. Her blood was bright blue rather than red because of the quantity of electricity she carried around in her body. Ellie was very brave and didn't even flinch as Neptune extracted her blood. Neptune then injected the blood directly into Daphne's neck, which Jock and Eugene held up for him, as she didn't have the strength to lift it herself whilst Pythagorus and Newton gave her a big hug of support.

Neptune did this three times before finally sealing up the hole in Ellie's tail with a special turquoise plaster. A few minutes later and to their immense relief, Daphne lifted up her head by herself just a few inches and gave them a very weak smile, the sparkle starting to come back into her eyes.

"I think we got to her just in time Neptune." said Jock as he stroked Daphne's back to try to warm her up.

"I agree." he responded as he too stroked Daphne's head. "Daphne" he told her "I'm afraid that we will have to leave you here for a while to recuperate. You'll feel much better in a couple of hours and we'll come and collect you when we have finished our search in the pearl beds and take you home."

"But," he added as an afterthought a few minutes later "I think I'll send a message to Artimas and ask him to get a couple of other electric eels to come and help you, just in case our search takes a little longer than we thought."

He then took out another water snail from his bag, and whispered some words in its ear in a language they could not understand. He then passed the water snail to Jock who threw it as far as he could up towards the top of the cliff and back home, in order to give the snail a head start on its long journey back.

As soon as the snail left Jock's hands, and as it flew up through the water, it seemed to grow bigger in front of them and it suddenly changed into a small crab. The crab grabbed hold of the edge of a rock, and sped up the cliff face at an amazingly fast pace back towards the school, and within a few seconds, had disappeared from view. The Octets had never seen this transformation before, so they were amazed!

They were just setting off again when Neptune suddenly felt the vibration of his phone ringing. It was Artimas, who had finally managed to get rid of both the doctor and matron. He had to assure them both that he was fine about a dozen times before he was finally able to convince them to leave him in peace. He had also been forced to swallow the medicine the doctor had insisted on prescribing him, so he was not feeling too happy and a little sleepy.

Neptune and Artimas spent the next few minutes updating each other on recent events. Neptune became quite worried when he learnt that it was Magnius disguised as Mr Magnihyde and Solumun that they were dealing with as he remembered hearing stories about Solumun as a child. Artimas was equally aghast when Neptune told him about the flooding in the mines and the electric force field and he was very frustrated by the fact that he couldn't be with them. He agreed to send out a search party to collect Daphne and a team of mine workers to start digging a tunnel through the landslide so that they could get home more easily.

Neptune meanwhile promised that he would phone Artimas as soon as they had some more news.

Chapter 24

Back at the school, Mr Pinkleton had arrived, and he joined Artimas in his room, bringing with him a selection of potions and powders he thought they might find useful. First Artimas arranged for some of the remaining sixth formers to go with some other electric eels to find and rescue Daphne.

They then enlisted Prince Henry's help to arrange for some mineworkers to commence digging a tunnel through the landside. They needed his help because of course it was still Sunday, which was everyone's day off.

Once this was all settled Mr Pinkleton made a cup of mint tea and they sat down to think.

Perhaps, Mr Pinkleton suggested, the two of them could help Neptune and the children by creating an invisible force field around them, but they were worried that their distance from the school could make this an impossible task and how would they know it had worked?

But it was the only idea they could think of so the two of them mixed various odd ingredients together and concentrated for the next couple of hours on the magic required to create such a force field. As you can imagine it was a difficult and complicated recipe as the ingredients had to be just right, so they had to concentrate very hard.

Meanwhile, Neptune and the others continued with their journey. The sandy floor quickly disappeared as they swam into a deep and wide open space and before long they couldn't see the land below them anymore. In front of them, and not very far away they could see rows and rows of wooden rafts which held wire baskets suspended below them in the water. Behind them and to both sides were more mountains, which stretched up high into the distance and which seemed to almost touch the roof. In the centre of the rows of wooden rafts was a large platform on which sat a machine that looked like a generator. Neptune explained that it acted like an immersion heater and it helped keep the water in this area warm.

The water did indeed feel different from the rest of the water in Oceana as the warmth made it feel much heavier and it was harder for the animals to swim through it. For some unknown reason the oxygen levels were also lower and it was more difficult to breathe, so they were all beginning to feel very tired and sleepy.

It also smelt fishy!

Ellie explained to them that this had once been a small sea water lake which had taken its water directly from the sea through the small channel they had just travelled through, and which had now disappeared under the landslide. Both the mountains surrounding it and the door which they had built at the entrance to the channel, had acted as a barrier to the rest of Oceana. As a result the pure water in Oceana was prevented from entering the lake and so it was still filled with salt water.

It was the only such place in Oceana, and great care was taken to ensure that the temperature and levels of salt and other minerals needed in the water were maintained. This helped to ensure that the oysters were happy and they continued to produce top quality pearls. It was the salt, she told them that made the water heavier and this was why it was more difficult to swim through.

Ellie then took them down deeper and a little further into the lake towards the oyster beds themselves. They soon found themselves surrounded by thousands and thousands of oyster shells, lying quietly in their wire baskets under the wooden rafts, swaying gently to and fro in the water. Occasionally, an oyster opened its shell just a little to see who was coming and what was making the noise, and so they caught sight of a flash of coloured light from the pearl growing deep within their shells.

Because it was so quiet they could hear a faint tapping noise every time an oyster opened and then closed its shell again and it almost sounded like rain drops gently tapping on a window. Although oysters don't have eyes, they have light sensitive spots which react to light making their shells open and so it almost seemed like the oysters were watching them.

Some of the baskets contained some very unusual oysters where the pearl was growing on the outside of the shells, and these baskets lit up the dim waters as the rays of light from above reflected off the oyster's pearls into the water. As you can imagine it was quite an eerie place to be.

"It is beautiful down here, but how an earth are we going to find the ruby if he's hidden it down here," asked Courtney looking around them despairingly, "there must be millions of oyster shells in these baskets, and it's so dim down here."

"Beautiful" added Sofia dreamily, who was transfixed both by the beauty and the quantity of pearls and oyster shells, which surrounded her. She was thinking of the exquisite and priceless jewellery you could make with the pearls.

"There is a small entrance, or should I say a shaft to the upper world in the mountains ahead, and I suggest we try that first." Neptune responded. "I also think we should try not to make a sound unless absolutely necessary so that if Magnius is down here he won't be able to hear us, but instead hopefully we will be able to hear him coming."

"What about the secret door you and Neptune were discussing earlier?" Bradley asked him quietly. "Shouldn't we be searching for that too?"

"I'm still not sure that it actually exists or even if it is located around here which is why I think we should check the mountains first." he replied.

"Why don't we split up again?" Jock suggested. "That way we will keep all of our options open and it should save time. The lake is not so big that we won't hear if some of us are in trouble, and as a last resort we can always use our mobiles."

"We agree." added Pythagorus and Newton in unison.

"I'm not sure splitting up is a good idea." Neptune responded thoughtfully. "Not after everything that has happened today."

But in the end and somewhat reluctantly, Neptune finally agreed to the plan. So Ellie with Francois, Rupert, Sofia, Courtney, Jock, Eugene and the two sixth formers Hugo and Tatiana set off to search the left hand side of the lake. This included the exit in the mountains near a palace that everyone already knew about.

Meanwhile, Pythagorus, Newton, Archie, Bradley, Verity and Neptune took the right hand side of the lake, which also included the area now buried under the landslide. But despite an extensive search by everybody which included touching every odd lump they found on the mountain walls, they found nothing of interest or unusual so they headed back towards the centre of the lake and the oyster beds.

Before they had started searching, Neptune had sent off a few more water snails around the lake and told them to watch out for any signs of Mr Magnihyde. As soon as they saw any sign of him, they were ordered to report back to him immediately. As soon as he let them go they also turned into crabs and scurried off in the water to keep watch.

Back at school and whilst they were searching, Artimas and Mr Pinkleton finally finished cooking up all of the ingredients they needed in Artimas' personal microwave and they began to cast the magic spell. The spell itself had taken some time to weave as they had to slowly extract the force field out of mixture, much like a spider spins a web, and it was a delicate and time consuming operation. Once properly spun, they then had to wrap the force field web around Neptune and the others individually and this could only be achieved by wrapping it around personal objects that belonged to them.

It was quite odd to watch them spin the force field web and then wrap the delicate material firstly around one of Newton's hockey boots and then one of Pythagoras's math's books! Artimas and Mr Pinkleton weren't sure if the force field was strong enough to protect them all but as they cast the spell, a warmth enveloped the twins as they travelled around the oyster beds and then the edge of the lake.

For no apparent reason, they suddenly felt quite refreshed and there was a hint of lavender in the water around them. What they couldn't see was the faint, spotty silvery glow, which had slowly appeared from out of nowhere and now surrounded them.

The magic force field was not completely successful and they couldn't quite make it invisible but as Artimas and Mr Pinkleton wrapped up the belongings one by one each person started to have an element of protection.

Jock and his team meanwhile soon arrived at the other end of the lake and found themselves looking down at the ruins of an old palace. The wooden roof had rotted away a long time ago to reveal tall, beautifully painted walls and tremendously complicated, but colourful mosaic floors. Gold and silver gilt covered parts of the building and there were marble statues strewn everywhere. Although the colours had long since faded from the walls you could still see how stunning they must have looked a long time ago when they were first painted.

On one side of the palace was a long terraced pathway, lined with two rows of marble lions, which led along the mountains edge to a large black, marble door. The door looked like it had been cut out of the rock itself, but it was in fact made out of a different material.

The door itself was huge, about the height of a house, and as they approached it towered high above them. In the middle of the door was a huge keyhole, which contained a black metallic key. To the side was a small box, which on closer inspection they decided contained an alarm system. Next to it was a large red sign that said "DO NOT TOUCH" in bold turquoise letters.

This looked like it was the exit through the mountains.

Jock and Rupert, who was now standing on top of Eugene's shoulders, checked the door for any signs of it ever having been opened. Jock had told them that as far as he knew this door was never used and remained locked at all times. It was protected by a sophisticated alarm system which sounded if anyone ever tried to open the door, which of course they never did as if the key or door was ever touched it also sent out an electric shock.

So they carefully checked every inch of both the door and the alarm box making sure that they never touched anything, but could find no signs of either the key or the door ever having moved or the alarm system being tampered with recently. In fact the silvery webs of the water spiders that lived there looked like they had been undisturbed for hundreds of years.

The others meanwhile searched the grounds near the door for any signs of Mr Magnihyde having been there but they also found nothing. So they left, convinced that he had not used this route to escape to the upper world, and headed back to wait by the entrance of the palace.

Whilst Jock and his team were searching the palace, Newton, Pythagorus and the others had begun to investigate the oyster baskets. The twins had never seen the oysters before and they marvelled at the immense range of colours that occasionally flashed through the shells, as the oysters peeped out at them.

In the centre of all of the baskets, they found a small wooden platform, which was obviously used as a workbench as it was littered with a number of small tools including clamps, microscopes and boxes of needles. The needles were used to inject the oysters with living tissue, which encourages the oysters to produce the mother of pearl nacre, or the inner shell and ultimately the pearl itself. It didn't hurt the oysters but as you can imagine it was a very skillful job and took years of training.

The sights and sounds that surrounded them enthralled them all. Climbing up onto the platform, Pythagorus was especially intrigued by the unusual tools he found, and in particular a round magnifying glass lying on the edge of the platform, whose edge was covered with hieroglyphics. He put out his hand and was just about to pick it up when Neptune yelled at him to stop. But the nearer his hand came to the object, the more Pythagorus wanted to pick it up and he felt himself unable to stop his hand from being drawn closer and closer to it, until eventually he couldn't stop himself from touching it. Neptune raced towards him to try to pull him away but he was too late.

As Pythagoras's hand closed over the magnifying glass he felt a strange heat come tingling through his hand and up his arm and within a few seconds it had covered the whole of his body.

At the same time a vivid violet light also crept across his body and he suddenly felt himself being overwhelmed by an intense hatred of his friends and especially his brother. Inside of himself he knew it was wrong, but there was nothing he could do about it as the feelings overtook him completely until he became a different person.

As the hatred raged inside him the magnifying glass began to shake in his hand and a violet laser beam suddenly shot out from its centre. Pythagorus turned towards his brother, his face by now the same violet colour as the beam, and distorted with hatred. Aiming the magnifying glass and the beam directly at him and with a blood curdling cry, he charged at his brother shouting "die, die".

Chapter 25

Bradley, Archie, Verity and Newton were initially frozen on the spot in shock at Pythagorus' words but just as he was about to hit Newton with the beam, Bradley and Verity managed to shake themselves out of the trance. Bradley jumped towards Newton and with a flying rugby tackle, pushed him off the platform into the lobster beds.

Verity meanwhile dived at Pythagorus's legs and knocked him off balance, and he fell backwards with a roar into one of the lobster baskets. Bradley and Archie then both dived on top of him and fought with him to try and take the weapon away from him. As they rolled around in the basket, the laser beam shot around in all directions in the water and a couple of times just missed Newton, who was now lying dazed at the bottom of another basket.

Neptune meanwhile placed his hands out towards Pythagorus, closed his eyes and began to chant seemingly oblivious to what was going on in front of him. As his chant grew louder a turquoise beam sprang out from between his hands and began to grow. Once Neptune felt that it had become strong enough he aimed it towards Pythagorus and his violet beam.

The violet beam suddenly seemed to sense Neptune's presence and deliberately turned itself towards Neptune's beam and a fight between the two of them began. Pythagorus had no control over the beam and he was unable to stop it from fighting. Neptune on the other hand had complete control over his beam and he was able to direct his beam by waving his hands around and chanting.

It was quite a sight to behold. The two beams soared high up into the water as they attacked each other. They sprang from left to right and up and down at such a speed that it was almost impossible to follow them. Lights and sparks and crashing noises sprang from them each time they collided and from a distance it looked like someone had lit a couple of sparklers together by accident.

As the two beams fought, Newton climbed up out of the basket and staggering back up onto the platform, saw what was happening, and ran towards Neptune begging him not to hurt his brother.

Pythagorus heard his brother cry out and something seemed to snap deep inside him as he suddenly leapt up gaining control over the magic that had taken him over and he dropped the magnifying glass on the floor. As the magnifying glass hit the wooden floor it smashed into thousands of pieces and Pythagorus began jumping up and down and shaking his hands, which were now burning from the heat of the beam.

At the same time, the violet beam itself disappeared as quickly as it had started and Neptune was able to open his eyes again and stop chanting. His own beam gently glided back down to him, bowed and then disappeared. All that was left was the magnifying glass which lay broken in pieces in front of them.

"What an earth was that?" Newton asked Neptune as he stared at Pythagorus, totally shocked by his brother's actions.

Pythagorus had stopped jumping around and was now sitting in a heap on the platform looking exhausted and disoriented by what had just happened.

"I think that was a little magic trick left for us by Mr Magnihyde." Neptune responded breathing very heavily from all of the exertion.

"It is called a magnilaser. As soon as it is picked up, it possesses the person holding it and it magnifies any evil or bad emotions that they may have inside them including anger or jealousy or resentment. It then turns that anger directly onto the object of their emotions with one and only one aim, which is to exterminate that object and it normally results in death or destruction." he continued. "It is very dangerous magic, and it has been banned from our lands for centuries."

"How did you and Pythagorus manage to overcome its powers?" asked Bradley as he too climbed back onto the platform.

"Well I think Mr Magnihyde underestimated the deep emotions that tie twins together from birth and it was that emotion, triggered by the sound of Newton's voice which finally helped Pythagorus overcome its evil powers." Neptune responded.

"Does that mean that Pythagorus hates me?" Newton asked quietly, bowing his head and looking down at his feet and away from his brother as he said it. He sounded shocked and a little sad as he said this.

"No, No Newton" he responded quickly, "it was his deep love for you that overcame the evil of the magic. He doesn't hate you at all." he added gently.

"So what made me try and kill my brother?" Pythagorus asked, as equally shocked as his brother.

"Probably something as simple as wanting the same aura as your brother," Neptune replied, "because if you remember that was the first time that you discovered something different about each other, and it probably made you vulnerable. Don't worry Pythagorus, the magnifying glass was looking for someone like you and there was nothing you could have done to prevent it."

"I'm sorry Newton" Pythagorus told him gruffly.

"Don't worry Pythagorus" his brother told him brightening up "it didn't work and we are both fine." and he smiled at him.

"How did Mr Magnihyde know about the magnilaser?" Verity asked Neptune.

Neptune sighed and then explained to them that Mr Magnihyde's real name was in fact Magnius and he told them the rest of the story he had just heard from Artimas.

"That explains it." commented Newton when he had finished. "We always thought he was a bit odd as a teacher."

Collecting themselves up, they then continued very cautiously to search the oyster beds, desperately hoping there were no more traps, but finding no sign of a hidden entrance or that anyone else had been there recently. Despondently, they headed to the palace where the others were sitting next to one of the marble lions, waiting for them.

Once they had all updated each other, the group sat around for about 10 minutes wandering what an earth they should do next as they had found no physical evidence of Mr Magnihyde anywhere even though he had managed to keep laying traps for them. As they chatted Ellie, Pluto and the seahorses relaxed close by and helped themselves to a few plants from the garden. They were starving!

Chapter 26

"Well," said Neptune eventually, "the fact that we have found no trace of Mr Magnihyde anywhere, and the fact that the roof has not yet caved in must mean that he is still here, somewhere in Oceana."

"And he must still have the ruby with him." he added sounding more positive then he actually felt.

"Yes, but where?" responded Sofia in a sulky voice. Although she knew that it was quite serious she was starting to get quite bored of this search and was feeling really quite tired from all of the exercise.

"Do you still think there is a secret door Newton?" Pythagorus asked his brother quietly. They were both leaning back on a couple of marble lions, a little way apart from the others. Pythagorus was still recovering from the shock of his attack on his brother, and he thought no one could hear them talking. He hadn't of course bargained for Neptune's excellent hearing!

"Yes" Newton replied, scratching his head as he spoke "I am absolutely convinced it exists, but I am not sure how we are going to find it."

"Why don't you see if you can feel Mr Magnihyde's aura?" Pythagorus suddenly suggested sitting bolt upright as he said it, "Do you remember you were able to see Peter when he was leaving Artimas' room even though you weren't actually looking at him?"

"Yes but he's not here now, so it won't work." responded Newton crossly, and he threw a pebble he had been playing with along the ground in frustration.

"True," replied Pythagorus thoughtfully "but there might still be a trace of him somewhere. You know in the same way that Ellie leaves a silvery trail behind her in the water. If you can't see anything maybe you can smell him" he added, "just like a bloodhound does."

At this, Newton immediately sat up and looked at his brother, a strange gleam in his eye. "You're absolutely right Pythagorus" he exclaimed. "I was able to sense his presence in the mines. Why didn't I think of that before? Come on, let's go and see what we can find." and he jumped up ready to set off.

Whilst the twins had been talking, and unbeknown to them, Neptune had heard their every word. So when Newton said "let's go", he interrupted them and shouted, "Wait a minute boys. This is such a huge area to cover; we need to somehow narrow it down."

They both turned and looked at him surprised. How on earth had he heard them talking they thought but he just grinned at them!

"If you ask me, I think the secret door is in the palace itself." suggested Courtney. They all stared at her as Neptune asked her what made her think that.

"Because the story you told us was all about a King and this is his palace." she explained crossly. "Surely a king would have his private entrance to the upper world, somewhere in his own palace."

"That's a brilliant idea Courtney." Pythagorus told her. Neptune nodded his head in agreement, convinced that she must be right.

"I think we should all stay out here and wait quietly," Neptune told them, "and allow Newton some space in the palace to sniff him out. I don't think we have much time left as Pluto tells me that one of the crabs has just spotted someone approaching the channel to the pearl factories. If it is Mr Magnihyde, as soon as he sees the landslide he will know that we are here and then we could be in serious trouble."

"How does Pluto know that?" asked Francois looking around him. "I haven't seen any crabs return."

"It's a form of radar" Neptune responded "and it's something that we humans can't see. Now off you two go quickly," he instructed Pythagorus and Newton," and good luck. Let us know as soon as you find something."

"Good luck Newton." the others added.

"Let me come with you?" Eugene asked them, just as they started to move away. "I am sure that I can help you both. I won't interfere," he quickly added. "I can act as a lookout or something." Neptune nodded his approval at this idea.

"Ok" responded the twins gratefully, glad to have an escort, as they were both feeling a little nervous. "Let's go" and the three of them jumped on their seahorses and headed off quickly towards the palace itself, whilst the others waited equally nervous outside.

As the three of them swam on their seahorses through the ruins of the palace, they did not know what to expect or where to look first. The palace was built on two floors and despite its age, and the number of years it had been under water, much of it was still in a fantastic condition. All of the pictures had disintegrated, and most of the furniture had long since floated away, but the marble and Alabaster statues still stood proudly in their places, together with the marble staircase which had once joined the two floors together.

The three of them searched the top floor first. They went through many bedrooms and bathrooms, but despite Newton closing his eyes tightly and concentrating as before, he couldn't feel, smell, or hear anything, so they floated down the staircase and began to check the rooms downstairs.

"This reminds me of pictures I've seen of the Titanic." Eugene whispered to Pythagorus as they searched the empty and silent rooms.

"Shush." Newton told him "I'm trying to concentrate."

There were fewer rooms downstairs so it didn't take them very long to complete their search. They went through living areas, kitchens and even some stables, but to Newton's frustration, he could still not sense or smell anything and there were no signs of Mr Magnihyde anywhere. So, they decided to head back to the others and give them the bad news.

As they headed back along one of the corridors they had already searched towards the main staircase, Pythagorus suddenly noticed something odd on one of the walls. He could see a long grey line stretching down the wall, just behind two large urns. When they investigated further, to their immense delight they found the faint outlines of a door, which they had not seen the first time they had travelled along the corridor.

It had been hidden by two large palm trees, which were sitting in the urns, and incredibly, after all this time were still living. They were the only two such plants in the whole of the palace, and although they had noticed them earlier, and thought it was rather strange, any further significance had been lost on them. It was only by chance that Pythagorus had looked again at the plants against the wall and noticed the faded grey line.

176

Eugene and Pythagorus jumped down off their seahorses, and pushed the plants aside so they could get closer to the door. The urns were very heavy and it was not very easy to move them but they finally managed to move one of them a few inches away from the wall so that they could just squeeze in behind it.

To their disappointment however, there was no handle on the door, and although they searched it thoroughly, they could see no visible means of opening it. They pushed it hard, but it was locked tight.

"I've got an idea," said Eugene excitedly "I'll call the others and hopefully, if we use one of the marble statues as a battering ram, between us we can force it open."

"Good idea." responded Pythagorus. "Don't be long," he added as Eugene jumped back onto Florin, his seahorse and dashed off to get the others, leaving the twins behind staring thoughtfully at the door.

Whilst Eugene was on his way back to get them, the others were sitting around talking quietly when Neptune suddenly felt something brush past his arm almost tickling him and he heard a small voice starting to talk to him in his right ear. It was one of the water snails that he had left at the edge of the channel.

Mr Magnihyde, he told him had now been spotted at the entrance to the channel. It had to be him the snail explained, because he had flown into a terrible rage when he saw the landslide and obviously realised that he had been beaten to the pearl factories. His route was blocked and he was now angrily combing the top of the mountains looking for another way into the lake, but it wouldn't be long before he found a way through and then found them.

Neptune sent him off again and told him to let them know as soon as he got into the lake.

It was at this point that Eugene came rushing back to tell them about the door and to get them to come into the palace to help the twins push it open. Neptune was very relieved to hear the news that they had finally found something interesting and they all rushed into the palace to join the twins.

"Can you feel any trace of him yet Newton?" Pythagorus asked his brother as he felt down the side of the door, looking for some kind of catch or lock.

The door was painted with a ballroom scene, full of dancers in brightly coloured dresses swaying across the floor. The picture blended in with the other murals painted across the walls in the corridor, which had helped to disguise the door when they had first looked at it. It was only the faint grey line that shone when you looked at it from one angle that gave the location of the door away.

Just then, and as Newton shook his head in despair, shoulders sagging because he still couldn't feel any trace of Mr Magnihyde, Pythagorus touched the hand of a man painted in the centre of the door. He was leading a beautiful young girl in a long silver ball gown to the centre of the room for a dance.

If Courtney had seen it first, she would have instantly recognised the king and the young girl from the legend Neptune had told them about earlier. But boys, being boys had not realised the significance of the painting!

Chapter 27

As Pythagorus pressed the ring on the king's hand they heard a large clunk, and the door slowly moved aside to reveal a vacuumed door leading into a large ballroom. Incredibly, the ballroom was still beautifully preserved, with some of the walls being covered in ancient and valuable paintings, and one wall was completely covered in handmade medieval tapestry wall coverings. On the floor was a beautifully polished oak floor – ideal for dancing!

Long red curtains draped down some parts of the walls and windows, and two large chandeliers hung down from a ceiling painted with gods and angels. Gold leaf glittered everywhere. It was quite a sight to behold and they both stood there, staring in disbelief as Eugene arrived back with the others.

They too were equally in awe of the sight of the ballroom. Even Rupert and Sofia were impressed!

"How on earth did you manage to find the way to open the door?" Verity asked them in astonishment.

"I just touched the hands of that man leading the girl to dance." responded Pythagorus as he pointed to the king in the picture. He still hadn't realised that it was supposed to be the king!

"It must be the king and the girl of the legends." stated Courtney firmly. She couldn't believe that they hadn't already recognized them.

"Yes, I think you are right." agreed Neptune. "But come on we must go into the ballroom and see if we can locate the secret door. We must hurry as I have just heard that Mr Magnihyde is close by and time is fast running out." He then led the twins and Eugene into the vacuumed chamber in order to enter into the room. There was only just enough room in the chamber for the four of them so the others waited behind ready to follow them.

As they entered the ballroom, both Newton and Neptune became conscious of immense emotions and of intense evil filtering through the stale and dusty atmosphere of the room. Newton felt bombarded by the evil particles that had been left behind and rubbed his forehead to try and brush them away.

"I'm sure that Mr Magnihyde has been here," Newton told his uncle as soon as they walked into the room, his eyes gleaming with excitement "and I'm sure we will find the exit in here somewhere." he added as he looked around the room for some sort of clue or even the door itself.

"I agree." replied his uncle and he motioned to the others to hurry up and come into the room." He then instructed Ellie, Pluto and the other seahorses to split up and to go and hide in the oyster beds. If they saw or heard anything, then they had to send him a message immediately. Jock and the other two sixth formers Hugo and Tatiana volunteered to stay with them and to look after them as necessary.

Jock then closed up the painted door behind them, so that Mr Magnihyde didn't realise that anyone had found the room and pushed the urn back into its original place. They then swam back to the oyster beds to hide and keep watch.

"How are they going to get a message to us, if we are in here, and they are out there?" Sofia asked Neptune curiously as the others began to search the room.

"Telepathy, silly." responded Rupert. Even he knew that! Sofia scowled at him and walked away to start looking around the room.

There were a couple of doors leading off the ballroom, so Neptune sent them off in pairs to explore. Sofia and Bradley had to climb up some stairs and immediately found themselves in a couple of bedrooms, which had been partly carved out of the mountainside. Through one of the long windows was a view of the gardens, and they could almost see as far as the oyster beds. The rooms were full of red and blue velvet drapes, tall carved four-poster beds and yet more paintings.

When Sofia peeped into some drawers and a wardrobe, she found that they were still full of exquisite clothes, all hand made with gold or silver threads running through them. Surprisingly they were all undamaged and there was even a faint smell of perfume on some of them. Some jewellery was left abandoned on the dressing table and Sofia was very tempted to take some home but Bradley glared at her when she started touching them so she didn't dare.

Courtney and Archie meanwhile found themselves in the dungeons, which were full of coats of armour, swords and long mail coats. In one of the rooms, they found a collection of fine wines. It was very dark and dusty down there and Archie kept sneezing. Suddenly, Courtney thought she spotted a spider coming towards them so they hurried back up to the others in the ballroom.

Eugene and Verity found themselves in some private living quarters, which were full of sofas, yet more paintings and amongst other things, a piano! Rupert and Francois meanwhile found themselves in a grand library, which was full of books and old manuscripts. They became so engrossed looking through the ancient books that Neptune had to send Eugene and Verity to find them as he had started to think that something had happened to them when they didn't come back to the ballroom.

Back in the ballroom itself, the twins and Neptune continued to search both the walls and the paneled floor for some signs of the secret door but to their dismay they found nothing. It was however obvious to them all, that this part of the palace had been left in a hurry, as whoever had lived there had taken nothing with them. It also looked like it had never been disturbed since that day, as wherever they looked there was a fine coating of dust and nothing seemed to have been touched.

As they all met up again in the centre of the ballroom, Newton continued to look around the room and kept finding himself being drawn to the huge ebony mantelpiece surrounding the fireplace on the back wall. Below it, and inset around the hearth were some white tiles covered in pictures of swimming dolphins and whales. Although it was beautiful, something about it just didn't feel quite right.

For example, there was not one speck of gold leaf painted anywhere on the tiles or the mantelpiece itself whereas everything else in the room was covered in gold. The dark dense colour of the wood was also at odds with the gold and yew furniture found in the rest of the rooms.

Then, he suddenly realised with a jolt that of course, it must have been placed there much later, obviously to disguise or hide something. This he felt sure was where they would find the hidden door.

He smiled to himself, pleased with his discovery.

Leaving the others, Newton approached the mantelpiece and began to carefully touch and search its surface for a switch or catch or some sort of lever. The others, who had been standing talking, suddenly realised what he was doing and rushed over to help, all getting in each other's way in the process, but they also found nothing.

"Stand back children and let me think. "Neptune suddenly instructed them and waved to them to come back into the centre of the ballroom "You are all getting in the way." he scolded.

As they stood back, Neptune studied the mantelpiece carefully but he also could see nothing. Then he suddenly called Eugene and Verity who were the only ones with some advanced magic training, to come and hold hands with him so that they could form an arc in the middle of the room facing the fireplace.

"Now look at the fireplace and then close your eyes," he told them all "and then concentrate as hard as you can on trying to see what is behind it."

But although they concentrated hard, nothing happened so he beckoned Newton and Pythagorus to join them to form a circle and told the others that they also had to concentrate very hard.

Including Newton and Pythagorus in the circle for some reason seemed to make all the difference, as this time they all became aware of an intense heat, and as the others watched, the fireplace began to slowly light up. At the same time, the ebony mantelpiece seemed to disappear under their scrutiny to reveal a glycon door leading to a hidden staircase. The stairs themselves were lit by series of candles and they seemed to lead away deep into the mountainside.

They had found the secret exit at last, and Neptune let go of their hands. Despite the fact that the circle had gone, the staircase was still visible to them all.

"What do we do now?" Pythagorus asked Neptune as soon as he had released their hands. He was longing to go up the stairs and investigate. "Why hasn't it disappeared again?"

"That is because the mantelpiece never existed in the first place." Neptune told them. "It was a vision created in our own minds by a magic spell to conceal the staircase from our sight. It is the staircase that is the reality not the mantelpiece."

"It was just a simple and yet very clever trick." Neptune added smiling.
"What we must do now," he continued, "is to set a trap to prevent Mr Magnihyde from escaping up the staircase so that we can catch him here in the ballroom."

"Now you must all hide behind the curtains and doors so that he doesn't see you when he first enters the room." he instructed. "As soon as he approaches the fireplace, we will all need to jump out and catch him. The element of surprise will be our saviour. I will hide on the other side of the fireplace, so that if you don't manage to catch him he can't escape up the stairs straight away without passing me."

"How will you get onto the stairs, and how can you hide from him?" asked Archie curiously. "We haven't found a way of unlocking the door, and anyway won't he be able to see you?"

Neptune just smiled at him knowingly and said, "You'll see in a few minutes."

Then he suddenly stopped smiling and for a few seconds, seemed to go into a deep trance as a look of panic swept over his face. Just as quickly, the look of panic disappeared and he came back out of the trance with a watery smile.

"I'm afraid, Ellie has just seen Mr Magnihyde riding through the oyster beds, and he should be with us within minutes," he told them "time is running out. Now quickly run and hide. Ellie says he looks very angry." he added grimly.

"How do you know that?" Archie asked him, stopping in the centre of the room, even more curious than before.

"I've already told you, "Neptune told him crossly, "telepathy. Now please hurry up and hide all of you." and with that he started to walk towards the fireplace.

"But how....?" Persisted Archie, but Bradley and Eugene grabbed him and dragged him towards one of the doors before he could say anymore. The others all ran and hid around the room.

"Newton, Pythagorus, come here quickly and help me." Neptune called out to them just as they were about to hide behind a pair of curtains. "I think I'm going to need your help."
" He then lifted up his hands towards the staircase and began to chant in Atlantian.

"What do you want us to do Uncle?" Pythagorus asked not understanding a word that his uncle was saying.

"Help me to create a force field which will stop Mr Magnihyde from immediately crossing through the fireplace to the stairs." Neptune told him.

"I will do the same from the other side. As soon as we have created the spell you can run and hide." And with that he continued walking towards the fireplace, chanting.

"But we don't know how!" Pythagorus told him desperately, grabbing hold of his uncle's arms to stop him from walking any nearer to the fireplace.

"Just look at the fireplace and repeat the words after me Newton, and concentrate hard. Pythagorus just help your brother." Neptune added. "I will tell you when the force field is finished." And with that he took one last step towards the fireplace and with a puff of smoke, he vanished and reappeared at the bottom of the staircase.

He continued to chant and as he did, a string of words seemed to appear in Newton's head, which he repeated as best as he could. Pythagorus held one of his hands tightly and tried to copy everything his brother said. As they chanted, Neptune seemed to fade away in front of them and a silver cloud seemed to grow from out of nowhere, becoming steadily thicker by the second.

They were right in the middle of creating the cloud and concentrating very hard, when suddenly there was a loud crash behind them, and Mr Magnihyde burst out of the chamber and almost fell into the room. As soon as he saw them, he came rushing towards them with his arms outstretched towards them. When they turned to look at him he roared in anger at them.

It was too late for them to hide now; he had caught them.

"Get down on your knees NOW." Mr Magnihyde shouted at them. "Don't you know who I am? I am Magnius, son of Lord Solumun."

"Now SHOW ME SOME RESPECT" he yelled.

With that, Magnius stopped in the centre of the room, raised his arms and hands towards them and seemed to grow to almost twice his normal size. At the same time he continued to shout at them, throwing words that they could not understand in their direction.

□

186

Chapter 28

Each word seemed to create a spark, which flew off in all directions and which stung them when they hit them. A drowsiness began to overwhelm them all, including everyone who was hiding in the ballroom. Despite the protection of the force field Artimas and Mr Pinkleton had created around them, and despite their best efforts to fight it they all quickly succumbed and one by one they fell down on the floor into a deep coma. Without the help of the force field, which unbeknown to them allowed them to keep breathing under water, they would have died.

But Newton was having none of this, and as the others began to fell onto the floor around him, he too raised his arms in the air, closed his eyes and concentrated on throwing back the sparks at Magnius himself. Neptune watched quietly from the staircase and continued, unnoticed, to whisper the words of the spell to create the force field which would prevent Magnius from leaving.

Luckily, he was too busy dealing with Newton to notice Neptune hiding at the bottom of the stairs. Newton did well and was able to deflect back a large number of the sparks before he too began to tire and he finally began to fall under their spell and sank down onto his knees. He had not yet been trained in this type of combat and had acted on pure instinct.

Back at the school, Artimas and Mr Pinkleton were sitting in his study both quietly dozing. It had been hard work creating the force fields around the twins and the others, and it had used up a lot of their energy so they were both having a quick nap. Artimas suddenly woke up with a start. In his dreams he had suddenly become aware of the fight between Magnius and Newton as unbeknown to them, the energy between them was throwing up flashes of light and tiny sparks. These had somehow travelled up out of the palace and through the water, rebounding off the roof and creating a musical note in the process. These notes reverberated through the water and could be heard for miles around them and it was this music, which had penetrated Artimas' sleep and had woken him up.

Artimas shook Mr Pinkleton awake and the two of them stood at the window, looking towards the oyster beds and listening to the music. As the music played out, a picture of the fight soon formed in their minds and they quickly realised what was happening. They both stretched out their arms in the direction of the palace and began to chant in order to create a second spell to send some of their magical powers and strength through the water to Newton to help him continue to fight. As their spell developed it too created sparks and its own musical notes which began to fly back through the water towards Newton crashing into some of the sparks being created by Magnius in their way.

The sounds of the competing music were now loud enough to be heard by some of the people of Oceana. Not knowing what was going on, they came out of their houses and just stood and marvelled at the beautiful music and the fireworks cascading from the roof which were being created by the flashes of light. They had never seen anything like it!

Back in the ballroom, Newton, who was on the verge of falling asleep, suddenly started to feel refreshed so he jumped back onto his feet and began to fight back again. Magnius growled in annoyance and spoke the words even faster so that now there was a fountain of sparks raining down on Newton's head. To the inhabitants of Oceana it was as if the music was coming to a grand finale and they watched and listened in awe.

Newton had initially been able to draw on an incredible strength seemingly from out of nowhere, which he had directed at Magnius. The magical spell sent by Artimas and

Mr Pinkleton initially renewed this strength, but in the end, they were too far away and by the time it got there, the spell was weak and so Newton finally succumbed to Magnius' spell. He sank again to his knees and then keeled over as he too fell into a deep coma. He had however been able to inflict a great deal of damage to Magnius, in the process and he was now considerably weakened.

Magnius stopped chanting and with a smile at his victory staggered towards the fireplace without paying too much attention to it, and attempted to cross over to the staircase. But, to his horror, he walked straight into the force field that Neptune had been able to construct and nearly knocked himself out. He fell back with a bang onto the floor in the ballroom hitting his head in the process. He sat up, slightly dazed rubbing his head in confusion and even more weakened than before.

At this, Neptune jumped through the fireplace and with his hands aloft began to attack Magnius with more magic, drawing away the rest of his powers. A shaft of light shot from Magnius' body into Neptune's hands which he then pulled and twisted and scrunched into a ball.

At the same time, Jock, Hugo and Tatiana, who had followed Magnius unseen into the palace had been watching everything from the safety of the corridor, jumped out of the vacuumed chamber and dashed over to help Neptune overcome him. As they had been hiding outside the ballroom, Magnius' spell had not affected them, and so they were able to hold him down until Neptune had drawn away every last particle of his powers from him into a tiny ball of light. He then tucked the ball into his bag and locked it up tight.

Magnius still struggled to get away, but Jock tied him up very tightly with a piece of rope and for good measure tied a scarf across his mouth so that he couldn't speak any more.

Neptune meanwhile sat back in the fireplace, exhausted and watched as Jock went round and woke up the others one by one, by spraying a silver liquid that he had brought with him onto their faces. Artimas had given it to him before he had left the school - just in case!

Pythagorus who was nearest was woken up first. He dashed over to Magnius and began to carefully search him. Magnius had tried to wriggle away but he was too tightly bound by the rope to move very far.

A few minutes later Pythagorus let out a whoop of joy- he had found the ruby, wrapped up in a small velvet pouch, which was buried deep within Magnius' jacket.

Magnius had obviously not expected to be caught as he had not hidden it away or protected it with any kind of spell. The others soon arrived and they began to dance around the room, singing and laughing and jumping with joy. All except Newton, that is, who despite all of Jock's and then Neptune's efforts to wake him up remained slumped on the floor in a deep coma.

"What's wrong with him Neptune?" Jock whispered to Neptune anxiously. The others hearing what he said, suddenly realised that there was a problem with Newton so they stopped dancing and listened just as anxiously to Neptune's response.

Neptune studied Newton carefully for a few minutes and then looked up at Jock with a worried expression. "I don't know why but I just can't seem to wake him up Jock" he told him sounding very worried. "I think Magnius most have hurt him a lot more than we realised. We must get him to Artimas as fast as we can. Only he will know how to save him." he added gravely.

Pythagorus burst into tears in shock. "Uncle is he ok? Is he going to die?" he asked him tearfully.

Courtney flung her arms around him to try and comfort him.

"I hope not Pythagorus," answered his uncle sounding very worried, "but I'm not really sure. We must hurry back to the school." He then told Bradley and Hugo to pick Newton up gently, and they carried him off to Ellie who was waiting outside the palace. The others pushed Magnius up on to his feet and escorted him outside, where they tied him over the back of Pluto, who would carry him back to the school.

They sped back home with mixed feelings. Elated that they had captured Magnius and the ruby, but panicking that Newton would not survive. It was a very subdued group that started the long journey back home.

Chapter 29

The first thing that Neptune did once they left the palace grounds was to phone Artimas to give him the good news about the ruby. Artimas and Mr Pinkleton had already realised that the fight was over because the music and lights had suddenly stopped and now there was just silence. They had strained to hear for other sounds, which could indicate that the roof was starting to crack, or that pressure was building up in the water, but to their relief they could hear nothing.

As soon as the music had stopped, Prince Henry had telephoned to ask Artimas if he knew what had created such a commotion and what was happening. He didn't recall ever hearing such sounds or seeing fireworks in the water before. Artimas was just about to explain everything to him when his phone bleeped and he realised that Neptune was trying to call him, and so he actually cut the prince off in mid flow!

Artimas listened intently as Neptune told him how they had finally captured Magnius and retrieved the ruby. He explained how Pythagorus and Newton had found a secret door leading to a hidden ballroom, which they had discovered behind a secret panel in one of the corridors. He then told him how Newton had fought Magnius hard and had nearly collapsed like the others. How Newton had suddenly regained his energies (Artimas smiled at this, knowing that this was as a result of his magic spell). But he had then collapsed again but not before he had managed to hurt Magnius and knock him down. How he himself had jumped out of the hidden fireplace and with Jock's help they had finally managed to overcome him.

But it was when Neptune explained about Newton's deep comma that Artimas became suddenly energised.

"Don't worry Neptune," he told him trying not to sound worried "just bring Magnius and the boy to me as quickly as you can and I will sort them both out."

"Have the miners been able to dig out a tunnel through the landslide yet so that we can get home that way?" Neptune asked him.

"I'm not sure," replied Artimas, suddenly stopped in mid flow. He had forgotten all about the landslide and the inevitable delay it would create. "I suggest you send a couple of your water snails to check things out your end. I will phone the miners and tell them to hurry up. We will see you all as soon as you get back."

"Well done." he added "Brilliant news!"

Artimas then rang Prince Henry back to give him the good news that both Magnius and the Ruby had been captured and how it had all happened. The prince was so pleased, that he immediately declared that the next day would be a Bank Holiday. He then rushed off to organise a party and of course to tell the King that everything was fine. Artimas decided not to mention anything about Newton at that stage as he was sure that he could wake him up once he could see him.

Meanwhile, Neptune sent off a couple of water snails ahead of them as scouts to find the best route home. They were all feeling very tired and hungry, as it was hours since they had last eaten and it was now quite late in the evening. As they approached the original entrance to the pearl factories, which was still blocked by the landslide they were delighted to be greeted by Daphne. She was recovering well from her ordeal and had been anxiously waiting for them with a couple of other electric eels who had not long arrived to keep her company.

When Daphne first saw them, she squealed and rushed over to them, talking non-stop in her silvery voice, but so fast they couldn't understand a word she said. She dashed over to Neptune and flung herself at him, wrapping herself and her tail around him to give him a big electric hug. To his embarrassment, she even gave him a big, slobbery kiss. For a few seconds he regretted helping her, but then he just laughed.

Once Daphne had uncurled herself and had calmed down, she told them that a team of miners had been digging through the top of one of the mountains close by, and they had just told her that they had nearly managed to tunnel out a small gap between the top of the mountain and the roof. Unfortunately, it was not very wide, so the seahorses would have to swim side wards and the others would have to crawl along.

Ellie, Daphne and the other eels would of course have no problem, but Pluto would have to be left behind because he could not fit through the gap. They had already agreed that a couple of the miners would keep him company whilst they attempted to widen the hole.

Daphne led them along the side of the mountains and then up towards the top of the roof, until they could hear the close sounds of banging. As they waited by the side of the mountain, treading water, and wondering how long they would have to wait, there was a loud cracking noise, and one of the rocks in front of them suddenly broke off and came crashing down in front of them. It just missed hitting Archie by only a few inches and he was by now starting to get a complex, having been involved in so many accidents in one day.

But all this was soon forgotten when they saw a black hat and then a head pop out from inside the gap left behind by the falling boulder in the rocks. It was one of the miners who had finally reached the end of the tunnel.

They were so relieved to see him that they all started to cheer; all except Magnius who began to mutter under his breath and ignored them. They were even more pleased when he opened up his rucksack to reveal a fresh supply of sandwiches, some drinks, and a flask of steaming coffee for Neptune and Jock. There was even some fish for the animals! It was an odd place for a picnic, but not surprisingly, even though the sandwiches were damp, everything tasted wonderful and it was soon devoured.

They were so busy eating and thinking of home, that they didn't pay any attention to Magnius still tied up on Pluto's back.

This was perhaps an unwise thing to do as his every murmur created a small bubble in the water, which ordinarily would have quickly evaporated but in this case remained intact, and floated gently away behind them.

"I'm afraid the tunnel is very narrow and there is only just enough room for you to crawl along on your bellies." the miner told them. "All except Pluto that is, who is far too big so I will stay with him until the tunnel is wide enough for him to pass through."

Sofia, Courtney and Verity all groaned. "Do we have to crawl?" Sofia asked, thoughts of a hot steaming bath coming to mind as she glanced at the steam coming from Neptune's coffee. "Isn't there any other way?"

"No" the miner told them. "Unless of course you want to wait here with me and Pluto for a few days whilst the other miners widen the tunnel?"

"No, no it's ok" Sofia replied, despondently. "I'll do it!"

Bradley and Hugo then proceeded to untie Magnius from Pluto's back and instead tied him between Ellie's humps.

They then strapped a still unconscious Newton onto Daphne's back as she had flatly refused to carry Magnius. They hugged Pluto goodbye, and one by one they began to crawl, or slither in Ellie's and Daphne's case along the narrow tunnel towards home. Magnius continued to mutter and in the close confines of the tunnel this was becoming very irritating, so Sofia tied her favourite Hermes scarf around his mouth, but even the combination of the two scarfs didn't completely stop him.

What none of them had seen, as none of them had looked back towards the oyster beds since entering the tunnel was the string of bubbles lying in the water behind them.

If they had studied them closely they would have realised that each bubble contained a word, and that the string was in fact a long line of sentences containing a secret message. Pluto, the other two electric eels and the miner who were busy talking to each other were also oblivious to the bubbles that had been left behind.

Neptune and Pythagorus were the last two to approach the tunnel, and as they entered the darkness, Pythagorus thought he heard the faint sounds of music breaking out behind them. But when he tried to tell Neptune, he told him that it was either his imagination or the sound of Pluto saying goodbye and he urged him to hurry up and catch up the others. So Pythagorus thought no more of it.

The remaining journey back to the school was uneventful and it wasn't long before the very welcome sight of the school's clock tower appeared in the water in front of them. A few minutes later, (or so it seemed!) they found themselves all crowded into Artimas' room. Mr Pinkleton, Artimas and Neptune were all talking at once and it was very noisy and crowded in the room.

A little earlier, Pythagorus, Bradley and Eugene had slowly carried a still unconscious Newton up to Artimas' room, and they had gently laid him across two chairs. Neptune meanwhile had pushed Magnius in front of him, almost forcing him to fall over in his hurry, and Magnius was now standing in the corner of the room ignoring them all and still muttering despite Sofia's scarf which was still firmly tied around his mouth.

Jock and Bradley had taken the seahorses, Ellie and Daphne down to the stables. They were all hungry and exhausted and in desperate need of some pampering. With the help of some of the other sixth formers they were soon all fed, watered and groomed. Ellie and Daphne then headed off for the Milky Bar and a well-deserved rest whilst the seahorses were tucked up in their boxes with some fresh straw and a blanket.

Within a few minutes they were all happily snoring, gently bouncing up and down in the water with each snore. The other seahorses however were very restless and unsettled but Jock was too tired to notice them, as he was more interested in returning to Artimas' room to find out whether Newton had now woken up. Some of the seahorses whined and pawed the floor as he left, but he just ignored them.

"Welcome back Neptune, welcome back children" Artimas told them as they entered his room, holding out his hands in greeting and beaming at them all. "I am so proud of you all, and I am so relieved to see you all back here safe and sound. And what a fantastic job you have done.

"Now where is my ruby?" he asked them anxiously

"Here it is" Pythagorus told him smiling. He took the ruby out of his pocket and handed it over to Artimas, who was by now trembling with relief and excitement at getting his precious ruby back safely.

"But what about Newton," Pythagorus asked looking at his brother who was still unconscious. "Is he going to be alright?"

"He will be fine" Artimas reassured him, "just as soon as I've sorted my ruby out." he added as he concentrated on the delicate operation of replacing the ruby back into the cradle on top of his staff. It was quite a complicated procedure as the ruby had to be lined up in exactly the right position before it would drop down into its casing, and it took Artimas some time before he succeeded. After all, it was the first time he had ever tried to do this!

Pythagorus became very frustrated as he watched Artimas fumbling with the ruby, so he wandered over to the window, which overlooked Plympton, and joined Mr Pinkleton who was gazing out thoughtfully at the view. The others were all standing in small groups around the room talking quietly, whilst Magnius continued muttering in the corner.

Artimas finally managed to slot the ruby back into his staff and with a triumphant whoosh, waved his staff around the room sending flashes of red light and tiny florescent dust particles shooting everywhere. Artimas began smiling at everyone and he suddenly looked ten years younger.

Once he was satisfied that the ruby was safely back in place Artimas bent over to study Newton who, still unconscious, was oblivious to everything that was happening around him. Using the staff, he steadily moved it up and down Newton's still body in long slow strokes. The ruby emitted a deep red glow, which as it touched Newton's body created a warmth, which slowly began to penetrate through his body and down into his soul.

The ruby produced so much energy that the room itself started to became very hot and the others all began to sweat in the heat. Newton initially seemed totally oblivious to the touch of the staff, but as the minutes ticked by; he slowly began to regain his colour and started to stir as Artimas' magic pulled him out of his deep slumber. The others watched the process, fascinated, and relieved to see that Newton was finally starting to wake up. It looked like he was going to be all right after all.

Whilst this was going on, Pythagorus, who couldn't bear to look at his brother, just in case Artimas' magic didn't work, continued to stare out of the window. As he stared he suddenly became aware of what resembled a cloud in the water, far off in the distance. A pretty white fluffy cloud. He was just admiring it slightly puzzled as it floated towards them, when he suddenly realised with a jolt that it was impossible for there to be a cloud in the water.

"What is that cloud over there?" he asked Mr Pinkleton who was still standing next to him but was now looking into the room watching Artimas. Pythagorus pointed to the cloud, which now seemed to be getting closer and closer by the second.

"I'm not entirely sure," Mr Pinkleton responded sounding very puzzled. "I've been watching it myself for the past few minutes and I don't think I like the look of it."

Neptune overheard their conversation and wandered over to see what had attracted their attention. He too looked very startled to see the cloud, but his gaze soon turned thoughtfully towards Magnius who was still muttering to himself in the corner. He stepped menacingly towards him and told him to shut up or else, but to no avail. Magnius ignored him and continued to mutter.

"I am not sure if I am imagining this but the cloud is starting to look more like a dragon or some sort of sea monster." Pythagorus said anxiously, as the cloud continued to approach them. It was getting bigger and bigger as it slowly headed towards them "Can you see it too, or am I imagining things Mr Pinkleton?"

"No it's not your imagination," Mr Pinkleton told him sounding even more worried, "I can see it too."

Chapter 30

"ARTIMAS" Mr Pinkleton suddenly commanded. "Come here quickly I think we have a problem. I think Magnius has somehow summoned Glucifer, and it looks like someone is riding her."

Artimas immediately stopped what he was doing and looked up at him aghast. "Pythagorus," he commanded, "come here and help your brother The rest of you children, go and help him." He then jumped up and dashed over to the window.

Luckily, Newton was now starting to wake up and Pythagorus only had to wait a few minutes before his brother opened his eyes and smiled. "I'm starving Pythagorus," he told him. "What's for dinner?"

"Trust you to only think of your stomach." Pythagorus responded. "Here," he added, helping him sit up, and he handed him a sandwich and a coke they had saved for him, which Newton soon demolished. As he ate, Newton stared at Magnius and he suddenly stopped muttering, as if silenced by the intensity of his glare.

"Are you alright Newton?" Courtney asked him in a slightly wobbly voice as she sat down beside him.

"I've got a bit of a headache but I'll be OK." he responded smiling at her.

Artimas meanwhile was staring out of the window as the cloud which had now transformed into "Glucifer" glided in the water towards them. Glucifer it turned out was a mixture between a flying horse and a dragon with a long spiky tail. Although she was pure white, and had a beautiful face, she was not at all angelic; in fact she was quite the opposite. In legends she was known as the white devil. She spat out ice rather than fire, and one look from her piercing blue eyes could chill a man's soul and turn him into an ice statue.

According to legends, she had been so wicked that an earlier prince had been forced to banish her from Oceana for eternity. No one knew where she had gone but legend said that she was locked away in a prison hidden deep down under the mountains. It had been so long since she had last been seen; most people thought that the stories about her were a fairy tale rather than a real story.

Although they couldn't see him properly, riding tall on Glucifer's back was Lord Solumun, Magnius' father. He was also dressed from top to toe in white, from his white leopard skin cowboy boots, to a pair of white sunglasses to reflect away the glare from Glucifer's coat. All around them was a thin white mist of evaporating ice created by the movement in the water from Glucifer's vast wings, which had helped disguise their arrival.

Sensing that there was a problem, some of the others gathered around the window to stare at them.

"Whatever you do," Artimas told them sternly, "when she gets closer don't look directly into her eyes or you will be instantly turned into ice. She sends out a beautiful sweet scent to entice you, and she has such a lovely face from a distance that it is difficult not to look. But you must ignore the urge." He added anxiously "Don't let it affect you."

"Where has she come from, and why is she coming here?" asked Archie nervously.

"I'm not sure." Artimas replied, "I have never seen her before, I have only heard about her from stories passed down the generations."

Mr Pinkleton nodded his head in agreement, and added, "She hasn't been seen for a couple of centuries, and the last legend talks of her being banished up into the upper world to live in an enclosed sea from which she could not escape. Her magic doesn't work in salt water."

"Do you think Magnius is calling her?" Sofia asked them, looking directly at Magnius who had started muttering again, and was now grinning from ear to ear, as he listened to their conversation.

"Oh gosh of course!" exclaimed Mr Pinkleton and he started to wave his hands at Magnius. "Why didn't I think of that?" He chanted a few Atlantian words and a few seconds later Magnius fell into a deep sleep. They then gagged up his mouth with another scarf and tied up his hands so that he could not cast a spell to destroy Mr Pinkleton's magic.

But it looked like Mr Pinkleton was too late to stop Lord Solumun as Glucifer seemed to have already found them and she was now gliding up the hill towards the school.

But as soon as the muttering stopped, Glucifer stopped dead in her tracks and shook her head from side to side and stamped her feet in temper, as it seemed that she no longer had a signal to follow. Now that she was so close to the school, they could clearly see the ice steam blowing from her nostrils and Lord Solumun's white hair floating in the waves behind them. He looked very angry.

It had also turned very, very cold in the room and some of them began to shiver.

"There is no point hiding. I know you are there," Lord Solumun shouted at them. "Now give me back my son." he demanded in such a loud voice that it seemed to reverberate around the whole school, causing even the bricks in the walls to vibrate.

Nobody answered.

"Give me back my son now, or you will all die." Solumun demanded again even louder, standing up on Glucifer's back and pointing his staff in the direction of the school.

"I think we ought to put up our shields Artimas," suggested Neptune quietly. "I don't like the look of this at all."

Artimas nodded his head in agreement, pointed his staff in the direction of the clock in the clock tower and muttered a few words that none of them understood. Whatever he said seemed to somehow press an invisible button in the tower as a few seconds' later, metal shields shot up to the roof, from deep within the seabed and enclosed the whole school in a protective shield.

Although the shields were metallic, they were made from a similar material to Glycon and they were also transparent, so they could see everything around them, including similar shields which were now also shooting up over Plympton. The residents in Plympton could see and hear Glucifer and they too were anxious to protect themselves.

As the shields shot up in front of him, Lord Solumun suddenly realised what was happening. He shook his own staff for a few seconds and aiming it at the school started firing with an orange laser beam at them, obviously intent on damaging the school. But, he was not quick enough, and the laser beams bounced off the rising shields in all directions, hitting and destroying things in their way, including a wall, some plants and parts of the road!

At this, Lord Solumun completely lost his temper, and he began shooting aimlessly in the water, firing at nothing in particular but still aiming to damage anything that got in his way and to frighten them. He also shouted some instructions at Glucifer, and she began to blow ice clouds at the shields. As the ice started to stick onto the shields it put a tremendous strain on the metal and small cracks began to appear on their surface, and they could all hear the shields groaning under the weight.

"He's hitting the roof as well as the shields Artimas." Mr Pinkleton whispered worriedly. "We must do something quickly to stop him, or he will destroy the roof as well as the school."

"Why don't you challenge him to a duel?" suggested Rupert, who had obviously watched too many cowboy films.

"Don't be silly." sneered Sofia, "How do you know he won't win?"

"Can't you cast some sort of magic spell?" asked Archie, "Which will make him go away. I don't like dragons." he added nervously partly hiding behind Courtney..

"Why don't we get on our sea horses and try and surround him and fight him?" added Bradley sounding very positive. "If we can catch Peter I am sure we can catch him."

"I just need to think." he added again thoughtfully.

"Why don't you offer him back his son, in exchange for our freedom?" asked Newton quietly who had by now joined them by the window as he was starting to feel much better. "Of course they'd have to promise to return back to the upper world, and never come back here again." he finished.

"Not a bad idea," responded Artimas nodding his head thoughtfully, "except I'm not sure they will just leave quietly now that they are both here. I think they are far too cross that their plans to steal the ruby failed and Lord Solumun seems determined to destroy us first."

"In that case," replied Newton, "you will have to talk to Glucifer and offer her a better life back here in Oceana if she changes sides. I'm sure she must be very lonely in exile and she probably misses having friends." he added sliding back down in the chair. He was still very tired after everything that had happened to him.

"What friends?" exclaimed Pythagorus and Bradley together in disbelief. "How can anything like that creature have friends?" they asked.

"If I remember the legends properly," explained Artimas suddenly looking more cheerful, "she did have some friends once, before a previous sorcerer corrupted her with his evil magic and made her the bad dragon she is now. But how can we talk to her?" he added hesitantly. "And does anyone remember who they were?"

Everyone kept very quiet and waited whilst Artimas paced around the room thinking.

"Oh but wait a minute. Of course, Newton." Artimas suddenly added thoughtfully.

"How very clever. All we have to do is talk to her in our minds just like we do with the other animals. Oh my. I'm not sure if we can communicate with her through the shields, but perhaps if I try this." he added mumbling to himself rather than to the others.

Artimas then turned around and facing Glucifer pointed his staff at her. He went into a trance for a few minutes as he called out to her, but nothing seemed to happen and she continued to fire ice clouds at them.

Meanwhile whilst they had all been talking, Solumun had jumped off Glucifer, adjusted his sunglasses and strode towards the school entrance. He was now standing within inches of the shield attempting to bore a hole through the wall with the laser beam from his staff. Glucifer was also concentrating all of her energy on another part of the shield with exactly the same purpose in mind.

She had stopped for a few seconds when Artimas first went into a trance, but she shook her head and carried on.

"I can't get through to her." said Artimas coming out of his trance and shaking his head. "The shields are too thick. Somehow I need to get closer."

With that, and before anyone could stop him, Artimas dashed out of the room, headed for the main entrance and jumped into the vacuumed chamber which would take him outside. They all watched him stunned as he swam up to the clock tower and then stood next to the clock, within inches of the shield. He was facing them with his back to the shield and Glucifer's icy stare and with his arms up in the air.

Solumun caught sight of him as soon as he came out of the chamber, and beckoning Glucifer, he dashed over to the clock tower so that they were now both facing Artimas, also within inches of the shield. Solumun began to laugh, as he invited Artimas to turn around and look into Glucifer's eyes and the water around the clock tower became thick with a sweet sickly smell, as Glucifer tried to entice him to look at her.

Imagine the smell of your favourite toffee or treacle and that is the sort of smell that wrapped itself all around Artimas. Artimas however ignored all of this, kept his eyes tightly shut and silently called out to Glucifer.

Again she seemed to stop what she was doing for a few seconds, and she shook her head in irritation as if she was imagining something annoying. But she soon ignored it and carried on boring a hole as before.

"I have to help Artimas." mumbled Newton as he suddenly jumped up on his feet. Courtney tried to stop him, but he was amazingly quick as if energised by the situation and before they could stop him, he too dashed out of the room to join Artimas, closely followed by Pythagorus and Neptune.

"You don't have to do this Pythagorus." Newton told him as they waited for the chamber to fill with water.

"Don't be silly Newton" he replied. "You are not strong enough to help him on your own. Now remember," he added, "you mustn't look at Glucifer whatever you do."

Chapter 31

Taking each other's hands, the two of them then swam quietly to the clock tower making sure that they always looked down and that they never looked at Glucifer. Neptune followed closely behind them. Luckily she was still busy concentrating on boring a hole in the shields in front of Artimas and so she didn't see them arrive.

The water smelt so sweet that they could almost taste the toffees and that seemed to draw them towards her, but somehow they managed to resist looking at her.

When they finally reached Artimas, he grabbed hold of them to stop them from floating away as there wasn't enough room for them all to stand on the clock tower. They held on to his hands and the four of them then began to call out to Glucifer as loud as they could, but of course still not making a sound.

This time Glucifer finally heard them. She stopped what she was doing, cocked her head to one side as she began to listen. Solumun however couldn't hear them and he continued blasting the shield, totally oblivious to what was happening right next to him and not initially realising that she had stopped. He thought that he could see a crack developing in the Glycon shield and he was busily concentrating on that.

With the twins help, Artimas and Neptune began to sing to her of the life she once had in Oceania. Artimas reminded her of her friends, and of the fun they used to have playing together every day. Especially with Honu her sea turtle friend. He talked of the free fish she received three times a day and of the lovely warm cave that she called home.

But it was when he started talking about her favourite strawberry milkshakes served at the Coral Café, that a single tear dropped from one of her eyes, and turned into ice as it hit her cheek. It sparkled with thousands of lights as a ray from Solumun's laser beam accidently touched it and everyone saw it, including Solumun.

Solumun suddenly realised what was happening when he caught sight of the tear and his bad temper turned into terrible rage as he turned on Glucifer demanding that she continue destroying the shield immediately, or he would personally kill her. For a moment she turned towards him and it looked like she was going to obey him, but then the song that Artimas was singing captured her attention again, and she turned away ignoring Solumun's rage.

With this, Solumun let out a terrible roar that could be heard for miles around. Turning his staff towards her he began to shoot laser beams at her head obviously intent on seriously hurting her. Glucifer calmly turned towards him, ignoring the pain from the beams, which were now tearing into her skin, bent her head down towards him until her face was within inches of his face, and just glared at him.

To their amazement, Solumun disappeared instantly to be replaced by a strange looking piece of ice. Glucifer turned away from him smiling, and continued to listen to Artimas's song. A few minutes later she started to join in!

"What do we do now?" whispered Courtney in awe.

"Where has Solumun gone?" added Bradley.

"I'm sure Artimas will let us know shortly what we should do." responded Mr Pinkleton who was still glued to the window watching the events unfold before him.

Artimas continued to sing his magical song, accompanied by a now smiling Glucifer as she swayed from side to side to the music. He slowly brought the song to an end and a few minutes later, she lay down on the ground and fell into a deep contented sleep, an even bigger smile on her lips.

Artimas finally stopped singing and for a few moments no one dared move or even breathe just in case she woke up. Neptune cautiously dropped down to the ground to check her through the shields.

"It's OK Artimas," Neptune shouted up towards Artimas a few minutes later "you can let the shields down now. Glucifer won't be any trouble and it looks like she's turned Solumun into a piece of ice. I'm going to take her back to her own cave as soon as she's had a nap!" he added grinning.

On hearing this Artimas pointed his staff at the shields again and they dropped back down into the seabed just as quickly as they had risen. The shields around Plympton followed suit and also dropped back down one by one.

Jock then led the others outside and they joined Artimas, Neptune and the twins who had already jumped off the clock tower and were all now standing next to a snoring Glucifer.

They walked around Solumun who was still frozen solid, his face pinched and contorted with anger. It was an amazing transformation and they were all a little worried that he was going to start melting any minute and start causing trouble again. Archie bravely touched him and as expected he felt cold and hard to the touch.

"What are you going to do with Solumun?" asked Francois eventually. "Is he always going to be transformed into ice because he would make a great statue for one of the squares in Plympton?" Some of them giggled at this thought.

211

"No, I'm going to take him away and put him a locked cell buried deep under my shop so that I can keep a careful eye on him," replied Mr Pinkleton. "I'm not sure if he can ever be defrosted, but I'll talk to Glucifer later and do some research in my old books to see if there is a known cure. He'll be quite safe with me and he can't escape. Don't worry." he added smiling at them all.

"What about Magnius?" asked Newton "What will happen to him?"

"We will lock him up in another cell under Mr Pinkleton's shop until Prince Henry has decided how he wants to punish him." responded Artimas. "He will probably banish him from our kingdom forever, just like his father before him, but I'll have to discuss it with him and the rest of the Privy Council first."

"Come on," he added "all this hard work has made me thirsty, so let's go in and have a cup of tea!"

So they headed back into the school, all talking at once. They were all feeling very tired by now but still excited after their eventful day. All except Neptune and Jock, who volunteered to stay with Glucifer until she woke up. After the events of the day, they certainly all slept well that night.

Once the excitement of the past few days had subsided, including the extra days holiday, school life continued as if nothing extraordinary had happened, and the Octets settled back into the normal activities of the last few weeks of the Christmas term.

Glucifer who was lying just on the edge of the school grounds remained in a deep sleep after Solumun was captured, and slept soundly for about a week. It took everyone in the school a few days to get used to the constant sound of her snores, but when she did eventually wake up and stop snoring it was amazing how much they all missed the noise she made!

Once awake, she was a different person from before and was no longer a threat to anyone as the enchantment of the past few centuries was now completely gone. In fact she was more like a pussycat then a frightening dragon!

Once she had woken up, Neptune, Jock and Ellie spent a long time talking to her before they allowed anyone else to approach her, just to make sure she was not going to suddenly become evil again. The octets couldn't wait to talk to her and kept trying to sneak out to see her but they were always stopped by Jock at the school gates.

About a week later Neptune called them all over to meet her and as they slowly and nervously approached her they were relieved to see that she was smiling.

"Hello" she greeted them in a voice that quivered like the strings of a violin. "Which one of you is Newton and which one is Pythagorus?" (She was obviously blind to the matching red hair).

The two of them stepped forward and she held out one of her claws, and to their amusement solemnly shook their hands! She felt so soft and silky when they touched her.

"Thank you so much for rescuing me from Solumun's black magic," she told them. "I owe you both my life, and if you are ever in danger then call me and I will come and find you, wherever you are."

She then handed them both a small silver scale, which she pulled off the edge of her tail. "All you have to do" she told them, "is to rub the scale between your thumb and forefinger and say my name three times and I will hear you."

"But," she added, "please only do this if you are in some mortal danger, as the magic will only work once. Do you understand?" She asked them looking at them both with an intensive stare. She almost looked scary again.

The twins nodded their heads and carefully hid the scales safely in their leather belts, where they knew they would be safe. Glucifer then beckoned them all to climb onto her back and she took them for a ride across the city to the pearl factories where they waved to the sleeping pearls before returning back to school. They were also pleased to see that there was no sign of Pluto who had obviously managed to get back through the tunnel.

Chapter 32

The following day, Neptune took Glucifer back to her old cave, which had not been touched since the day she left and still contained all of her belongings Even her favourite books were still sitting on her bookcase although they were covered in a thick white dust and smelt a bit musty. She quickly settled down into her new life, making friends with Ellie and Daphne and was often seen meeting both them and Honu for a drink of her favourite milkshake at the Coral Café.

The seahorses were exhausted and still a little unsettled after their adventures so Jock and Neptune decided that the inter house seahorse races scheduled for the following week should be postponed until the Easter term. Bradley and Pythagorus were very disappointed but instead they concentrated on pampering the seahorses and helping them settle back down into their normal routine. Jock even allowed them to bring their seahorses milk chocolate drops, which were much more interesting than carrots!

Both the end of school concert and the school play were however still on schedule for the last day of term. Francois and Sofia spent almost every spare hour practising their parts for the play. Archie had learnt his words almost immediately, but Francois was struggling with his part, and needed a lot of help. Bradley and the twins kept trying to skip rehearsals to ride on their seahorses, but Miss Zephyr always seemed to bump into them just as they were trying to escape and they were dragged back to help. It was as if she had prior knowledge of their escape routes, even though they fled a different way each time!

Finally, but swiftly, the last week of term and then the last day arrived. Because their parents had to travel such a distance to the school to see them, the school play always immediately followed the concert, which in turn followed a morning of speeches and prize giving. The concert itself was scheduled to start immediately after a special lunch in the great hall with all of the pupils and their parents and there was great excitement as the pupils waited the arrival of their parents.

To the twin's delight, even their father Tim was able to come to the school, as Ellie took him a special gas mask and some oxygen, and Katie held his hand and helped him swim to the school entrance. He was the first non-Atlantian person to come to Oceana and he had been invited in honour of the twin's success in retrieving the ruby and saving Oceana.

After the speeches, which were amazingly boring, the twins had just enough time to show their parents around the school before the gong rang for lunch.

The concert went very well and Miss Clang was delighted with their performance. No one made a mistake or sang out of tune, and Courtney's and Rupert's surprise duet at the end, which they had been secretly practising, was a great success and brought tears to the eyes of Miss Clang and some of the parents. Miss Clang became very flustered at the applause, twisting her hair into even more awkward angles in her embarrassment.

The other Octets were impressed by Courtney's sweet soprano voice which had come as a complete surprise and they cheered them both for ages when the concert had finished.

After a small interval, which to everyone's delight even included a cream tea, came the school play.

It was just about to start, when to their surprise Prince Henry suddenly appeared with Princess Katrina, his younger sister, to watch them. He greeted Artimas and Neptune like old friends, and they soon settled down in the best seats at the front of the hall to watch the performance.

Princess Katrina sat next to Neptune and they soon became engrossed in conversation, whispering to each other and giggling as the play progressed.

Sitting directly behind Neptune was Miss Rethless looking her normal gaudy self in a tangerine and lime green spotted dress. Throughout the duration of the play, the Octets could see her from the side of the stage glaring at Princess Katrina's back as she whispered to Neptune.

The school play of Romeo and Juliet started very well. Archie confidently strode across the stage in his green breeches, clutching hold of his sword and looking as if he had always lived on the stage. He had no problem acting out his part. Francois, who was initially very nervous, looked just as good in his outfit and once he had overcome his initial stage fright he seemed to fill the stage with his presence. He was so good that everyone soon forgot that it was just a school play and fell under the spell of the tragic love story, which unfolded in front of them.

Things were going brilliantly until the balcony scene. Miss Zephyr was using some artistic licence, and had swapped around their roles in some of the crucial scenes. So it was Juliet, played by Alexandra that had to climb up and down the vine to the balcony to snatch a kiss from the waiting Romeo. The vine was entwined around a ladder which reached to the top of the stage. They hadn't practised this scene using the actual set before, It wasn't until Alexandra started climbing, looked down and froze, that they found out that she was afraid of heights.

Luckily, Jock was holding onto the bottom of the ladder hidden from view and he was able to catch her when she fainted and started to fall off the ladder. Miss Zephyr and Jock looked at each other and panicked for a few seconds until Sofia, who was the understudy, stepped in from the wings and climbed down the vine towards Francois to continue with the play.

Sofia was brimming with excitement, although she tried not to show it, because of course just before the play ended and as she lay dying on a slab of marble, Romeo and Juliet shared a last lingering kiss. When the kiss finally came, it was with a real explosion of fireworks and she felt like she had just won the lottery. Francois was as usual oblivious to the effect the kiss had had on her and couldn't understand why, at the end of the play she was dancing around the back of the stage, whooping with joy. It was quite out of character. The audience cheered and clapped, as they had loved every minute of it.

"What did you think of the play dad?" Pythagorus asked his father proudly after the play had finished. "Weren't Francois and Archie brilliant? We share our rooms with them."

"It was great, despite the fainting incident." Tim replied smiling. "The acting was superb and both Archie and Francois have a great acting future ahead of them." he added.

"Katie my dear, it's good to see you again." interrupted Artimas as he approached them all smiling, holding his arms out in greeting. "You must be so proud of your boys."

"I am, we are." Katie replied, smiling at Tom.

"I don't know what we would have done without them." Artimas added.

Artimas then left them, climbed up onto the stage and addressing them all, thanked all of the pupils and teachers for working so hard all term. He wished them a happy Christmas and a good holiday and then added that he looked forward to seeing them all again next term.

"But before we go," he finished smiling. "We must not forget the events of the past few weeks and the amazing capture of Magnius, Lord Solumun and the Ruby of Life by Neptune, Jock, Eugene, Verity and of course, the Octets. I'm sure you will all agree," he continued looking in their direction as he spoke, "that they deserve a vote of thanks, and in particular Pythagorus and Newton deserve special thanks for their immense bravery and observation."

"If it wasn't for their sheer courage and determination," he continued "we would not be standing here now. With that in mind, I've invited Prince Henry to present them all with a special Oceana award for bravery."

Prince Henry and Princess Katrina then stepped up onto the stage whilst Artimas beckoned Pythagorus and Newton and the others to come and join them. The Octets looked at each other in astonishment. Nothing had been said earlier on in the prize giving about the Ruby, so they hadn't expected anything like this.

"Let's go." said Bradley suddenly taking charge, and he led them all up onto the stage.

Both Artimas and Prince Henry shook their hands one by one as they were presented with gold medals cushioned in deep turquoise velvet in small ebony boxes. When they looked at them closely, they saw that the medals had a picture of Prince Henry emblazoned on the front, whilst their names, the date and "In honour of saving our world" were printed on the back. Even Neptune and Jock received an award, but they were presented to them by Princess Katrina with a shy kiss on their cheeks. (Miss Rethless looked furious at this point!)

The whole of the school and their parents all clapped and cheered and stamped their feet as they were presented with the awards, with the loudest cheers saved for the twins. They were all very embarrassed by the attention, but they felt very proud.

After the presentation Prince Henry and Princess Katrina left for home, and Pythagorus and Newton took their parents back to their study room to show them where they lived and to collect their suitcases. Pythagorus immediately opened the floor in their living room and took great delight in introducing Tom to their seahorses Goldie and Koi, who were patiently waiting for them.

To his amusement, they seemed to know how important Tom was to them and they proceeded to show off with an impromptu display of summersaults and line dancing on the ocean floor! Tom was overwhelmed by everything he saw and when they finished he told them that he thought they were both beautiful. Goldie and Koi bowed to him as if to say thank you.

They all then headed back to the main entrance hall to meet Ellie and Neptune for their return trip home. They were really pleased because Neptune was coming back home with them for Christmas. The entrance hall was packed with departing children and parents and it was very noisy as they were all calling out goodbye to each other, but although they looked everywhere, Neptune was nowhere to be found.

The twins searched for ages for him, until they eventually found him squashed up against a wall under the stairs by Miss Rethless. She was throwing caution to the wind, and was trying to persuade him to come to her house instead for Christmas, but to no avail. As the twins approached, Neptune used their arrival as an excuse to move away from the stairs and gratefully fled back with them to the main entrance. Up until then, he had been oblivious to the fact that Miss Rethless had a crush on him and he hadn't known how to respond to her invitation. It had been quite a shock for him!

Within a few minutes they were all settled with their bags in Ellie's carriage and she swam up into the water and headed towards the exit tunnels and home. As they passed over Atlantia, they caught sight of Daphne and Glucifer, sitting drinking at the Coral Café. As soon as they spotted Ellie, they leapt up into the water to join them and swimming either side of her, they provided them all with an escort out of Oceana.

It wasn't long before they found themselves back on the beach under the cliffs at the bottom of their village. Although it was early evening, the sun was still shining as they emerged from the water and it was still a beautiful but a little chilly day. It took the twins a little while to adjust to the bright light and the sunshine, the cold and the taste of the fresh air. It had been a long time since they had experienced it all and they hadn't realised how much they had missed it!

Pythagorus and Newton gave Ellie a big hug, and then waved goodbye as she slipped down into the water and headed back to Oceana.

"See you next term" she called out to them in her tinkling voice as she left.

Once she was gone, the twins quickly climbed up the cliff stairs, eager to get back home. They suddenly felt homesick and couldn't wait to see Silky their cat and meet up again with their friends. As they arrived at the gate to their cottage, they were delighted to find their friends Harry and Billy waiting for them. Billy was throwing a cricket ball up in the air, whilst Harry was dribbling a football along the ground.

"Hi Pythagorus, Hi Newton," said Billy as he greeted them. "isn't it great to be on holiday from school?"

"Fancy a quick game of football before it gets dark?" added Harry.

"Can we please mum?" pleaded Pythagorus and Newton in unison. "We promise we won't be long."

"Be off with you before I change my mind." replied Katie smiling. "Tea is at 7pm, so don't be late." she added.

"Thanks mum." they replied, and they were both soon gone. Life was back to normal at home, and it was as if they had never been away. Oceana and their school suddenly seemed like a far off dream.

Printed in Poland
by Amazon Fulfillment
Poland Sp. z o.o., Wrocław